CHICAGO
ASSAULT

CHICAGO ASSAULT

RANDY WAYNE WHITE

WRITING AS CARL RAMM

OPEN ROAD

INTEGRATED MEDIA

NEW YORK

Cover design by Andy Ross

ISBN: 978-1-5040-3516-3

This edition published in 2016 by Open Road Integrated Media, Inc.
180 Maiden Lane
New York, NY 10038
www.openroadmedia.com

CHICAGO ASSAULT

ONE

Just minutes before the assassin fired, James Thornton Hawker realized that, instead of arriving late for an exclusive penthouse party, he had arrived early for a flesh orgy.

It was a party hosted by Chicago's very rich for Chicago's very beautiful.

Hawker knew he didn't fall into either category. He wondered why in the hell he had been asked to attend.

He had been invited by Saul Beckerman. The multimillionaire Saul Beckerman. The Saul Beckerman who was the ruling fist behind a chain of jewelry stores that crisscrossed the nation. The short, portly Saul Beckerman with the expensive toupee, the gaudy clothes, the gaudy cars, the gout-red face, and the backslapper's guffaw.

Beckerman was an acquaintance. Not a friend.

Even so, Hawker had always found him open and likable. Beckerman had grown up poor on Chicago's tough South Side. A quick little Jewish kid who had learned the hard way to survive in a neighborhood ruled by poor Irish thugs.

Beckerman was no fool. Instead of trying to fight the bullies, he used his wits to prove himself invaluable to them. He was inarticulate, uneducated; but he was smart enough to know that hustle and hard work can make up for almost any shortcomings.

Beckerman had one goal as a kid: to work his way out of the ghetto. Money became his ticket, tough business deals his vehicle. He climbed over backs and stepped on faces.

Business ethics were a luxury of the rich.

Beckerman kept right on ramrodding until he had made it to the top.

Hawker had met Saul Beckerman about ten years earlier at the annual awards banquet where Hawker was presented the Lambert Tree Award for Valor, Chicago's highest honor for a cop.

Beckerman was considered wealthy even then. Even so, his ghetto background was easy to read. In his speech. His dress. His raw jokes. His loud laugh. Hawker remembered thinking that he tried way, way too hard to fit in with his more refined business associates.

There was something both comical and pathetic about him. He was like a kid in a candy store: nervous but happy.

Everything seemed to impress him out of proportion. He had a terminal case of a ghetto kid's sense of inferiority. The award impressed him. Hawker impressed him. And the ceremony had almost reduced him to tears.

"Anytime you need anything, anything at all, you just come see Saul Beckerman," he had told Hawker solemnly after the ceremony. "Anything I got is yours. We both come from the same shithole, eh? We both worked our asses off to get out. We both know the score, right? These other bozos, they know how to hold their teacups and that sort of shit, but guys like you and me know something more important. We know how to fuckin' *survive.*"

Then Beckerman did something that had both touched and surprised Hawker. He had slipped his watch off his wrist, jammed it in Hawker's hand, then pivoted away, teary-eyed.

It was a slim gold Rolex. Even then it was worth a couple of grand. It was so beautifully made that Hawker rarely wore it.

Hawker had seen Beckerman off and on over the years. Never socially, though. So Hawker was a little surprised when he returned from a trip to the west coast to find the embossed invitation waiting at his little apartment in Bridgeport.

Along with the formal "You are cordially invited . . ." was a scrawled note from Beckerman:

Hawk—I got some important business to talk about. May need your help. Saul

So on a Saturday night in September, Hawker climbed into his midnight-blue Stingray, the vintage classic he had rescued from police auction, and cruised down Archer through the old Irish section. He picked up the Stevenson Expressway, east into the city. On Lake Shore Drive he turned north, wheeling easily through the lights and noise of downtown Chicago.

There was an autumn balm in the wind off the lake. The wind mixed the musk of fallen leaves and Canadian streams with the industrial stink of asphalt and foundry stacks.

Souped-up cars loaded with teenagers weaved in and out of

the suburbanite traffic. Late-night window-shoppers and club-hoppers roamed the sidewalks.

The party was at Beckerman's penthouse apartment. The apartment was a plush cell built into one of the marble and mirror-windowed skyscrapers that loomed over the city and Lake Michigan.

Hawker left his car with the parking attendant, then rode a sterile elevator to the twentieth floor. When he rang the bell, a black butler dressed in a white tuxedo swung open the double doors. The suite was done in marble and metal. Ultramodern. It was done so tastefully that Hawker knew Beckerman had either hired an interior decorator or left the furnishing up to his young and lovely wife, Felicia.

The room was crowded with a strange mixture of middle-aged men and young women. The women looked like they had driven straight over from Hefner's Playboy mansion.

There were blonds and brunettes, and one particularly sultry-looking negress. The punk look was in, and most of them wore their hair ratted or butch, styled in careful disarray. It was a night for formal attire, and their dresses were built to display, not cover. The girls seemed to be competing, to see who could show their breasts most spectacularly.

The men were big-business types. Expensive suits. Loud laughter through a plume of cigar smoke. Big glasses of bourbon being sipped through glazed smiles.

An army of Boise speakers pounded out gaudy jazz, and people yelled to converse above the din. Even so, Hawker could sense an awkwardness in the room, the uneasiness of strangers thrown together with unfamiliar plans.

The uneasiness didn't last long.

Hawker found the bar and took an iced Tuborg as far away from the speakers as he could get. There was still no sign of Saul or his wife, so Hawker sipped his beer and watched.

When the men at the party weren't belting down drinks, they were fetching drinks for the girls. Things were loosening up. There was the sound of wild laughter as the black girl climbed onto the shoulders of a chunky, balding man with a bright tie.

He paraded her around the room as she gulped a martini. When the drink was finished she tossed the glass away, then stripped her blouse up over her head and hurled it into the admiring crowd. Her breasts were heavy onyx, glistening with sweat.

The men clapped and cheered—and worked harder at their drinks as the other women began to step out of their dresses.

There were about a dozen females in the room, and soon they were all topless or completely naked. When the men began to huff and stumble out of their suits, Hawker knew it was time to find his hosts, give his regrets, and get the hell out.

The black girl had dismounted. She eyed Hawker from across the room, then padded through the staggering couples to the corner where he stood. She was down to sheer white bikini panties now, and her black pubic thatch was visible beneath them.

"How 'bout it, honey?" she challenged demurely, fingering the buttons on his sportscoat. "I'm all heated up and got no one to play with."

Hawker looked over her shoulder. "You're in luck. I think your friends are choosing up teams right now."

7

"Yeah," she said, pressing her bare breasts against him, "but I don't want to give these to anybody but you."

"I can't accept any gifts that won't fit in my pocket," said Hawker. "And those definitely will not fit."

Across the room, he had spotted Saul Beckerman's wife, Felicia. She wore a sleek white evening dress, and her raven-black hair tumbled spectacularly over her shoulders. Felicia's jaw was clamped tight, and her eyes blazed. She did not look happy.

Hawker handed his empty Tuborg bottle to the black girl. "Sorry," he said. "Company rules."

The bottle crashed to the floor as Hawker walked away.

He had met Felicia Beckerman only once before, at some civic function where everyone was too busy being polite to have a good time. She had struck him then as being an unlikely partner for Saul. For one thing, she seemed too bright. Too sure of herself. Too confident in her role of the modern woman to waste her time on a guy as crass as Saul.

Saul had money. And men with money usually end up with beautiful women. But Hawker had always expected Saul to end up with one of the brassy beauties. A gum chewer. A bleacher of hair and master of profanity. A loud dresser and louder talker.

But Felicia was Ivy League. She was quiet dinner parties and tasteful clothes. She was ballets and charity balls. She was everything Saul wasn't, which was no doubt why Saul had selected her as his mate.

The puzzle was, why had she selected Saul?

Hawker was at her elbow before she noticed him. There was a quick look of recognition in her eyes as he held out his hand.

"James Hawker, Felicia," he said. "We met—"

"Yes, Mr. Hawker. I remember our meeting well." Her face was tight and she seemed preoccupied. She released his hand quickly and kept her back to the activities in the living room.

"Is Saul around?"

There was an edge to her laughter. "Yes, *what* has happened to dear Saul?" She sipped at the martini she held. "But, really, Mr. Hawker, don't feel obligated to stand on formalities." She shrugged toward the people behind them. Someone had switched out the lights, so all you could see were ghostly tangles of bare thighs and breasts, and the sweating, heavy faces of straining men. "It's not required that you greet your host before jumping out of your clothes. Please feel free to enjoy yourself. After all, these are modern times. And we're all modern adult people, no?"

Hawker took her elbow and turned her toward him. She refused to meet his eyes. "Save the tone of contempt for your bare-assed friends in there, Felicia—"

"They're not *my* friends—"

"I got an invitation to a party. From your husband. On the invitation was a note saying Saul might need my help. That's why I'm here. I don't like parties to begin with. And group sex interests me about as much as a piece of communal toilet tissue. So spare me the glib rejoinders."

Taken aback, her eyes widened slightly. "Oh . . . I'm sorry . . . but—"

"And it's your party to begin with, Felicia. So if you don't like what's going on, the last place you should make your feelings known is to one of your guests." Hawker pivoted to go. "Tell Saul I've had a *grand* time—"

"Wait," she said quickly. "I'm sorry. Don't go."

She grabbed Hawker's elbow. Her lovely lips opened as if to speak, but then she lost control. Her face crinkled, she shuddered, and then the tears began to flow. Hawker stood for a moment, feeling awkward and stupid. Finally, he did the only thing a man can do when a woman begins to bawl. He pulled her head onto his shoulder and patted her gently.

"I shouldn't have snapped at you like that," he said lamely.

"No, I deserved it," she said, sniffing. "Christ, everything has gone so rotten. I don't even know what I'm saying half the time anymore." She turned away from him, rubbing her fists at her doe-brown eyes.

"The party was Saul's bad idea?" Hawker offered.

"Yes. And his ideas seem to be getting worse and worse lately. But this tops them all. He invited his most important business connections from across the country. He wanted to impress them. He read an article in one of those tawdry men's magazines of his that sex parties were the rage. It was an accepted way for wealthy businessmen to relax. Saul has never been what you would call tasteful, but at least he had good business instincts. Most of the men in there are married. Maybe even happily married. They're going to wake up in the morning feeling cheap and silly. They're going to hate themselves for weeks to come—and they'll end up hating Saul for much longer than that." She shook herself as if trying to awaken from a bad dream. She smiled weakly at Hawker. "How about escorting a lady out onto the balcony? I could use some fresh air."

Hawker smiled. "Sure. It's beginning to smell a little sweaty in here."

She chuckled weakly. "I'm going to have the place sterilized in the morning. If I'm still here in the morning."

Hawker took her arm and led her through the shadowy tangle of bodies. The record had stuck, and the stereo hammered out the same buzzing bass chord over and over again.

A feverish silence had fallen over the participants. There was a pile of naked bodies in the middle of the room. One man's eyes bugged slightly as a blond girl knelt over him, her head sliding up and down in rhythm to the record. The negress had found two playmates. She lay on the couch, her head thrown back, eyes in glassy ecstasy as the men sweated over her.

Hawker slid open the glass doors, and they went outside into the chilly September air.

Below, city lights twinkled. Toy cars and toy people moved through the streets. Lake Michigan was a deeper darkness between sky and horizon. White running lights and an amber flasher pulsed through the night as a tug pushed a barge toward Canada.

"God," Felicia Beckerman whispered. "It feels good out here. Clean." She took a cigarette from her handbag. The perfect lines of her nose and high cheeks were outlined in the flare of the lighter. She exhaled deeply, as if ridding herself of tension. "For the first time in a while, I think I might be able to survive the next month or two."

"More sex parties, you mean?"

"Not if I have anything to say about it." She allowed herself to smile briefly. "But it's more than that. It's Saul. Something's wrong with him. Something seriously wrong."

"You mean Mr. Beckerman hasn't been on his best behavior?"

She studied Hawker in silence for a moment. "Don't patronize me, James. I know what Saul is. I knew when I married him. He's rough and he's crass. I didn't love him. I told him that, but he said it didn't matter. But I did *like* him. Below that rude exterior of his is a truly kind and gentle person. Ours was a marriage of convenience. I'm the only child of two very dear people who have both suffered very serious health problems. It ruined them financially. I was desperate to help my parents, but I didn't have the way or the means. And then Saul came along. Dear, dear Saul. He courted me like a lovesick teenager. I told him my troubles. He made me an offer. Almost a business offer. If I married him, neither I nor my family would ever have to worry about money again. He was both kind and convincing. I thought it over for a long, agonizing twenty seconds. If I had to be a whore, I at least wanted to be a highly paid whore." She smiled thinly. "But the joke was on me. Saul had no interest in me . . . *that* way. I think he wanted to try on our wedding night, but he just couldn't bring himself to risk . . . failure, I guess. He was like a scared little kid. Maybe that's why he shows such bad taste with his crude jokes. And this party. Sex terrifies him. He has no idea of what's acceptable and what isn't."

She looked deeply into Hawker's eyes. "So I've been a kept woman these last four years. And I've never regretted it." She hesitated for a moment, as if slightly embarrassed. "Not from the business standpoint, anyway."

Hawker nodded, wondering why she had chosen to tell him

all of this. Maybe it was because she felt he deserved some explanation. Or maybe it was the empty martini glass on the railing.

"You said, *was* a marriage of convenience. Why the past tense, Felicia?"

She studied the glowing eye of her cigarette for a moment. "Because, for the last two months, it's as if the man I married no longer existed. Something is seriously wrong with Saul. He won't talk to me. He keeps telling me that I'm safer if I don't know. He can't be involved in anything illegal. He has too much money to bother with taking risks. But he's scared, James. I can see that. Someone or something has scared him terribly—"

The glass doors slid open, and a voice interrupted. "So this is where you two guys have been hiding!"

Saul Beckerman pushed the doors closed and stood grinning at them. The plump, swarthy face bulged above the tuxedo. "James, God damn it, it's about time you visited your old buddy!" Beckerman pumped his hand as Felicia studied the Chicago skyline, ignoring them. "Hey, James, you ain't out here trying to steal my best girl, are you?" The little man winked and exploded with nervous laughter. "I got a dozen of Chicago's finest inside. Yours for the asking."

"Those ladies are a little too open for my taste, Saul."

Beckerman laughed loudly. He seemed anxious and ill at ease. He made small talk for a while. Hawker noticed that he was sweating. It couldn't have been more than forty-five degrees outside, and the wind was colder. Beckerman also kept checking his watch.

Finally Hawker interrupted. "You said you wanted to see me about something important, Saul?"

Beckerman nodded quickly. He looked at Felicia, and Felicia turned quickly to go. "Wait, honey," Beckerman said, studying his watch again. "I got a little business to take care of first. Maybe you can entertain James for about twenty minutes? I just got to go down the hall for a bit. How 'bout it?"

"Sure, Saul," she said in a monotone.

Beckerman wagged his finger at Hawker, grinning. "But keep your hands off, you big Irish lug. You can look, but don't touch." He hugged Felicia roughly and added, "Watch this guy, babe. Word around town is he likes the chicks. Talk to you in a few minutes, Hawk!"

He banged Hawker on the shoulder and left the doors open behind him.

It took Hawker a moment to realize that Felicia was crying again. Weeping softly. "See what I mean?" She groaned. "He's like a mouse who's trying to pretend the cat isn't after him."

"Seemed like the same old Saul to me," Hawker lied.

She shook her hair back, fighting to regain control of herself. "You don't have to be polite around me, James. I remember the first time I met you. At one of those horrible luncheons. You were very polite there, too. I watched you out of the corner of my eye. For some reason, you give off the feeling of all those weird intangibles: confidence, tact, discretion. I remember thinking how nice it would be for a man like you to take me into his arms and just . . . just *hold* me. To make me feel like a woman again, instead of like a . . . damn museum piece, an object for public display."

"I'm flattered," he said. "I mean that."

She took a step toward him and touched his arm. "I want

14

you to be more than flattered, James. I want you to take me away from this. I want you to take me away from my life . . . for tonight, at least. Saul is so preoccupied lately, he won't even miss us. I've been the sterling, faithful wife for too damn long. I want to break the contract. I want to break the contract . . . with you . . . tonight."

She fell into Hawker's arms, and he stroked her hair tenderly before holding her away. He shook his head. "I make it a point not to mess with married women. Especially women married to people I know."

"It's a night for breaking rules, James."

"Not for me it isn't, Felicia."

She took a deep breath, steeling herself. "God, how funny I must be to someone like you. The rich, sex-starved wife. Is that it?"

"All you need is a portable vibrator and a nasty little poodle to complete the picture."

That struck her as funnier than it really was, and she began to laugh. A full-bodied, alto gust that seemed to make her feel much better.

When the laughter subsided she held out her hand. "Thanks," she said. "Thanks for not letting me make a fool out of myself."

"Believe me, it wasn't easy saying no. You are a very beautiful woman, Felicia. And under different circumstances it would be me trying to steal *you* off into the night."

"And thank you again—for returning my ego intact." She shrugged and rested her arms on the railing of the balcony. "And who knows, someday things may change. Someday, something might even happen to—"

Felicia never finished. The wind swept the dull *ker-whack* of the gunshot to them through the darkness.

There was a terrified scream.

Hawker swung around just in time to see the woman's eyes grow wide with shock and horror as the body of Saul Beckerman tumbled off a balcony beneath them, flailing, spread-eagled, his scream like a fading laser of sound, falling, falling, falling toward the asphalt nineteen stories below. . . .

TWO

Hawker grabbed Felicia by the shoulders and swung her away just before her husband hit.

Her face was frozen in shock. "My God," she whispered. "My God . . . that was . . . that was . . . *SAUL!*"

His name escaped her lips in a low wail.

Hawker pulled her inside. He fumbled for the switch, and the overhead neons blinked on. There were shouts of drunken protest from the naked people on the floor. The black girl was still on the couch. Hawker grabbed her by the arm and jerked her away from the man who had mounted her.

"Get your hands off me, man. You got no right—"

Hawker shook her roughly. "Shut up," he said in an even voice. "Shut up and listen. Get some clothes on. Find some brandy. Then take Mrs. Beckerman to the bedroom. Don't let her go near that balcony, understand?"

Hawker didn't wait for a response. The man who had been with the black girl was in his mid-fifties. He had neatly trimmed silver hair and was in surprisingly good shape. He looked like

17

he was probably respectable and reliable under different circumstances. Hawker grabbed him by the arm. "Are you sober enough to take charge here?"

"Hey—what . . . yes, of course—"

"Then get these people out of here. Mr. Beckerman's been murdered. Call the police as soon as you can."

"Murdered? My God—"

Hawker shoved his way through the living room and out the double doors. As he sprinted down the hall, he drew the customized Colt Commander .45 from the shoulder holster beneath his jacket.

The elevator was not in use. Hawker ignored it. He threw open the door of the stairwell and ran down the steps three at a time.

He stepped carefully into the hallway on the nineteenth floor. He could hear the low sound of voices. Anxious voices. Hawker moved toward the suite beneath Beckerman's apartment.

The door was cracked open. The voices came from inside.

Hawker hugged the wall as he moved toward the room. When he was about ten yards away, two figures bolted from the room. Two white males in their late twenties or early thirties.

One was holstering a revolver beneath his gray sports jacket as he ran. The other carried an ugly little automatic in his left hand.

"Freeze!" Hawker held the Colt Commander level and ready in both hands as he yelled.

The man with the automatic spun, his eyes wide with surprise. He busted off three wild shots. The automatic popped with the sound of books slapping together. The third shot ricocheted off the wall above Hawker.

Hawker squeezed off one careful round. In the narrow confines of the hallway, the explosion was deafening.

The slow .45 slug smacked through the man's chest and sent him skidding backward, as if on ice.

Blood coated the white marble floor.

"Get your hands against the wall," Hawker yelled. The second man was frozen near the elevator, right hand inside his jacket. "Move!" Hawker commanded. "Hands against the wall—now!"

Slowly, the man turned toward the wall, hands high.

Hawker stalked toward him. The man had black curly hair and the damaged, aged face of a drug user or alcoholic. He kept glancing over his shoulder at Hawker—or at the apartment where they had just killed Saul Beckerman.

Hawker kicked the man's feet wider. "Nose to the wall, asshole," he said evenly.

"You a cop?" the man demanded.

"No. But I'm the guy who's going to blow your ears off if you so much as sneeze."

"You got no right to be doing this, man. You're no cop. You got no right—"

Hawker smacked him in the back of the head. The impact knocked the man's nose against the wall, and his nose began to bleed.

"*Shit!*" the man hissed.

"Idle talk makes me real grumpy," Hawker snapped. "Keep it in mind. That's why you're going to tell me why you killed Beckerman. You're going to tell me first, and then you're going to tell the cops—"

"I hardly think so," interrupted a strange voice from behind Hawker. Hawker's head swung around. The door to the apartment had been quietly pulled open. A squat, broad-shouldered man with a beefy, red face stood in the doorway holding a Smith & Wesson Air Weight .38.

"Kindly toss your gun away," the man commanded. *"Now."*

Hawker bent and placed the Colt on the floor near his feet.

"Now kick it away, like a good lad."

The man had a light Irish accent. But there was the calm edge of the trained killer in his voice, too.

Hawker kicked the gun away.

"Christ, Kevin," whined the man with the bloody nose, "what took you so long?"

"Just straightening up inside the apartment. It pays to be careful, don't you see. Billy's dead?"

The man with the bloody nose retrieved his automatic and turned toward Hawker. "Yeah. This son of a bitch blew him away." He pointed the gun at Hawker's head. "Now I'm going to kill you, you bastard."

"By all means," said Kevin calmly. "Make it quick, lad. We've still got to find a back way out of here and meet our pickup."

"But first I'm going to bust his nose," said the kid, "just like he busted mine."

It was a mistake. Hawker knew it, and at once felt some hope of escape. The Irishman, Kevin, knew it, too, and he tried to stop the kid.

"Don't hit him, you stupid fool! Just shoot him and be done with it."

The kid lowered his weapon and threw an overhand right at

Hawker's face. Hawker stepped under the punch and slammed his fist deep into the kid's solar plexus.

The kid made a *whoofing* sound as Hawker swung him toward the Irishman. The two men collided in a tangle of arms and legs.

Hawker dove for his Colt Commander. Two slugs exploded off the floor beside his head.

Hawker's right hand found the cold weight of his weapon, and he rolled onto his back, firing four rounds in rapid succession.

The kid was slammed backward into the wall. His little automatic spun wildly in the air as his face melted into black gore.

The Irishman clutched the spreading stain on his jacket, as if trying to stop a leak. His .38 fell from a quivering index finger as he slid down the wall.

Hawker got to his feet and went to the Irishman. He was dying, and he knew he was dying. A helpless smile crossed his pale face. "The stupid kid," he whispered. "A stupid opening to give you."

"Yeah," said Hawker. "It was pretty dumb." He knelt beside the dying man. "Why did you do it?" he demanded. "Why did you kill Beckerman?"

The Irishman studied the blood seeping from between his fingers in disbelief, then looked at Hawker. "Orders, of course. We had orders."

"Whose orders, damn it? Who would have you hit a guy like Beckerman?"

Blood bubbled from the Irishman's lips with the soft chuckle. "And why would I be telling the man who . . . who killed me?"

His head slumped sideways, eyes frozen wide.

He was dead.

The hydraulic whine of the elevator told Hawker the police were on their way up. He knew he had to hurry.

Quickly he went through the pockets of the three corpses. He didn't know why Saul Beckerman had been killed, but it had all the signs of a professional job.

Hawker didn't like professional killers. But he had even less affection for the organizations that hired them.

Hawker had spent the last year fighting such organizations. With the help of his wealthy friend, Jacob Montgomery Hayes, he had, in fact, dedicated himself to fighting any group anywhere in the country that preyed on innocent people.

Saul Beckerman wasn't a close friend. But, in an odd way, he had won Hawker's respect. Saul's note had said he wanted to see Hawker on important business.

This business? The business that had ended his life?

Maybe. No—*probably*. Beckerman knew Hawker's reputation as a tough cop. The best, until he resigned because of all the bureaucratic bullshit that made dealing effectively and legally with crooks and killers damn near impossible.

Beckerman knew he was in trouble, and he had also known that Hawker might be the one individual who could help him.

So this was to be Hawker's assignment: Save Saul Beckerman from unknown killers for unknown reasons.

Hawker hadn't even been hired, and already the assignment was blown.

But it wasn't too late for Hawker to go after the organization that had hired the killers.

Retained by a dead man?

Sure, Hawker thought as he surveyed the three corpses. Why not?

Sometimes justice was the most demanding employer of all.

Quickly, he went through their pockets. Money. Cigarettes. No identification.

They had been careful. Damn careful. It was to be expected. They were professionals.

But in the jacket pocket of the Irishman, Hawker did find something. It was a crumpled piece of paper. On the paper were written two names and two addresses.

One was Saul Beckerman's.

The other was a name that stunned Hawker.

It was James O'Neil of 2221 Archer Avenue.

Jimmy O'Neil was James Hawker's best friend. . . .

THREE

Hawker got to Jimmy O'Neil's place at just after one A.M.

He had spent more than an hour dealing with the police, answering questions and trying to calm the beautiful Felicia Beckerman.

The first plainclothes cop to arrive was a man Hawker knew well. He was Boone Chezick, a heavily muscled, dour man with whom Hawker had worked many times.

They had had their differences. In fact, they had spent quite a few years hating each other's guts. But, a few days before Hawker resigned from the force, they had come to a platform of truce. They still didn't like each other much. But there was a grudging respect between the two men.

In the last year, Chezick had been promoted from lieutenant to inspector, and transferred to the detective division.

Inspector Chezick. Homicide. It sounded strange to Hawker.

Chezick stepped out of the elevator. He wore an almost threadbare blue suit beneath his cheap trench coat. There were three cops in uniform behind him. Except for a slight widening of the eyes, he showed no surprise at seeing Hawker.

He considered the three dead men, then looked at Hawker. "Still trigger-happy, huh, Hawker?"

Hawker smiled. "It's a reflex action. Whenever someone starts shooting at me, I start firing back."

"Did you kill the guy splattered on the pavement downstairs, too?"

"Saul Beckerman?"

"I don't know his name. We haven't scraped his I.D. out of the cement yet."

"No. I didn't kill Saul. These guys did."

"You're sure?"

"I was standing on a balcony on the twentieth floor with Saul's wife. We heard a gunshot. A moment after we heard the shot, we saw Beckerman tumble off the balcony below us. I came running down. These three guys were just coming out of the apartment. When they saw me, they opened fire."

Chezick grunted and gave orders to the uniforms. As they went to work with their cameras and their tapes and their chalk, Chezick approached Hawker.

"Let's have it," he said. "Your weapon."

Hawker drew the Colt Commander and handed it to the inspector butt first. Chezick wrapped it in his handkerchief without touching it. "You got a permit, I suppose."

"I do."

"Self-defense, right?"

"Right."

"You have any witnesses?"

Hawker nodded toward the corpses. "None you could hold a conversation with."

Chezick deposited the Colt in his trench coat pocket and took a step toward Hawker. His jaw was tight and his tiny, pale eyes were squeezed to slits. "The boss man isn't going to like this, Hawker. He still hates your guts from when you were on the force. The press had a way of making him look like a fool, and you look like a hero. He's going to make us go over this thing with a fine-tooth comb. If there are any irregularities at all, he's going to try to nail your ass. He'd love nothing better than to see you playing one-on-one with rat shit in the state pen." Chezick sniffed and scrubbed at his nose with a huge fist. "He thinks you're trigger-happy. That's why he says he canned you."

"I resigned, Chezick. Check the records."

For the first time, Chezick allowed himself a thin smile. "Yeah," he said. "I know. And I don't blame you, Hawk." He pulled a notebook out of his back pocket and flipped it open. "So tell me what happened, old buddy." His smile broadened. "And you'd better make it good."

So Hawker went over the story again. He went slowly and carefully, as Chezick scribbled in his notebook. Hawker's only lie was the lie of omission. He didn't tell him about Saul Beckerman's request for help. And he didn't tell Chezick about the note he had found in the Irishman's jacket.

"Then you didn't actually see these three men kill Beckerman?" Chezick questioned.

"How in the hell could I?" snapped Hawker. "We were on the next floor—like I told you."

"So, actually, you just *assumed* they killed him?" Chezick sniffed and checked his notes before he gave Hawker a probing look. "I don't suppose you came running down here and found these three guys just coming out of the apartment and blew them away? You know, shoot first and ask questions later? And then, maybe, staged all the rest of this? Fired their weapons, wiped the prints off, then set 'em up. Could you have done something like that, Hawker?"

Hawker felt the blood rising in his face. "Sure, I could have set them up. Any cop can set up something like that. But I didn't."

"The commissioner's going to figure the worst."

"I don't give a damn what he figures. It happened just the way I told you."

"They killed Beckerman, and you interrupted their escape?"

"Right."

"No doubt in your mind about that?"

"God damn it, Chezick, don't treat me like some stupid rookie! I told you what happened. That dead Irishman over there practically confessed when I asked him why they had hit Beckerman. Remember? He said, 'Why should I tell the man who killed me?'"

Boone Chezick shrugged and put his notebook away. "The lab reports better confirm every single inch of your story, Hawker. Beckerman better have been murdered, and these bloaters better have powder burns on their hands—from their weapons. Because if it doesn't match up, I'll be coming after your ass. You can bet the damn bank on that. The commissioner will see to it. So, until we get everything checked out, don't—"

27

"I'm not going to leave town," Hawker interrupted coldly. "Anytime you want me, Chezick, you'll know where to find me."

Hawker turned toward the elevator and didn't look back.

Hawker stopped at the late Saul Beckerman's penthouse before heading for his car.

Except for another team of uniformed cops and Felicia, the apartment was empty. Those who had come for the sex banquet had vanished. Hawker wondered how they felt, how the lethal finish to their plunge into the modern world of fun-love had affected them.

The image of a dozen wealthy, middle-aged businessmen scattering bare-assed toward the parking lot almost made Hawker smile.

Felicia was in her bedroom, lying on a massive circular couch. Her room was neat and immaculately decorated. There was a walk-in closet, a Jacuzzi whirlpool near the sunken tub, and a series of pen-and-ink drawings on the wall.

The pen-and-ink drawings were studies of gnarled oak in winter. They gave the room a faintly masculine air. They seemed to shout out her loneliness.

Everything else bespoke a wealthy, refined—and independent—woman. All woman.

She lay on the couch with her forearm thrown across her eyes. A policeman was in attendance. He sat on a chair by the bureau. He looked bored. He seemed to recognize Hawker. He nodded.

"I need to give the doc a call, anyway," the cop said as he rose and headed for the door. "I think she's going to need a shot or something."

Hawker knelt down beside her. "How're you doing, lady?"

She shook her head wearily. "It really happened, didn't it? Saul really is dead."

"Yes. It happened."

"My head's roaring. Everything seems to be coming at me down a tunnel. There's an air of unreality about me . . . you . . . this moment."

Hawker touched his hand gently to her arm. "It's called shock. It's nothing to be afraid of. A doctor will be here soon."

Her face trembled as if she were about to cry, but she didn't. She studied Hawker for a moment. "Just before . . . just before Saul left, I was about to say that I wished something would happen to him. Something to make me a free woman. My God, it's like it was—"

"You had nothing to do with it, Felicia. Every married man and woman who has ever lived has made that same secret wish at one time or another. Few of them mean it. And I know you didn't mean it."

"But I did want to be free!" she cried.

"Even if you did, it had nothing to do with Saul's death. Remember that. You have absolutely nothing to feel guilty about."

She nodded noncommittally. "I've just been lying here thinking how damn lucky I was you didn't let me seduce you. I don't think I could have stood knowing that Saul died while I was—"

Hawker touched his finger to her lips. "Enough," he said. "You need to rest."

"You're going?"

"Yes."

She propped herself up on one elbow, brushing the silken brown hair off her face. "Please call me. Please."

"I will."

"James? Saul didn't commit . . . I mean, was he—"

Hawker had opened the door. He stopped and turned. "He was murdered, Felicia. I killed the men who did it."

"I'm glad," she whispered. "I feel better knowing that."

FOUR

As Hawker climbed into his midnight-blue Stingray, something the Irishman had said touched one of the memory electrodes. Something about having to hurry because they had to meet their "pickup."

The apartment building was bordered on the north and south by connecting alleys to Lake Shore Drive. On a hunch, he cruised through the first alley.

Not much to see. Three cars, all parked and seemingly empty.

Hawker turned onto Lake Shore, then immediately turned left into the second alley. More parked cars. Garbage cans. Two winos sat on a bench, propped against each other, trying to stay warm in the cutting Lake Michigan wind.

Their driver had probably headed for home at the first sound of sirens.

No, the driver wouldn't have headed for home. These guys were professionals. They would have had a second pickup point. Or maybe even a safe house.

Whatever their alternate plans were, Hawker knew there wasn't much hope in a random, one-man search.

Chicago is a big, big city.

Hawker turned onto Lake Shore again and headed for Bridgeport.

Jimmy O'Neil lived in a narrow, two-story brownstone house, yard-to-yard, driveway-to-driveway, with hundreds of other brownstones.

Even so, Hawker had no trouble finding it. As he parked on Archer in front of the house, he wondered how many times he had walked up that sidewalk into the old brownstone. How many summer afternoons had he spent there as a boy, shooting the bull with Jimmy O'Neil, or doing homework, or making grand, boyish plans?

Through elementary school and high school, he and Jimmy had been more than best friends. They had been almost like brothers. They had too much in common for it to be any other way.

Both were Irish, second-generation Americans with their parents fresh from the old home soil. They were the same age, and they had both loved sports.

Their fathers—old Ed Hawker and rough and husky Blair O'Neil—were both cops. Damn good cops, if everything Hawker heard was true. And they both liked to sit together on the porch on summer evenings over tall stories and taller glasses of beer.

So it seemed preordained that Hawker and Jimmy would be best friends.

And they were. Everywhere Hawker went, Jimmy went. Their Little League team won the city championship. In high school football, both were all-state selections: Hawker as a running back; Jimmy O'Neil as a tackle. They had played together, ate together, fought together, and dated girls together.

Inevitably, as happens in all boyhood friendships, graduation, jobs, weddings, and the solitary process of aging separated them. They saw less and less of each other.

Jimmy had been filled with the passions of the "Irish Cause" for as long as Hawker could remember. So he wasn't surprised to hear that, upon graduation from Notre Dame, O'Neil headed straight for Northern Ireland with his law degree.

There were rumors that O'Neil had joined up with the Irish Republican Brotherhood and was fighting England's despised Orangemen, which wasn't at all hard to believe since Blair O'Neil was, like Hawker's own father, a dedicated Fenian.

O'Neil had the connections to do it. And he had the brains. And, as Hawker and everyone else in Bridgeport knew, the IRA depended on the support of Irish-Americans—for money, weaponry, and manpower.

For nearly five years, Hawker heard nothing from O'Neil, save for an occasional scrawled note. There was never a return address, but the postmark was always somewhere in Ulster.

Then one day, O'Neil returned to Chicago. There was no fanfare, no prior announcement. He simply reappeared, as if he had gone to the store for milk and was late getting back. Hawker was still married at the time, but O'Neil's wife had long since divorced him. O'Neil opened a law office but seemed to pour most of his money—and his time—into opening a bar. A fine Irish bar, of brass and polished woods and rare corned beef sandwiches, called the Ennisfree.

The Ennisfree became the acknowledged collection center for IRA donations. Hawker had also heard that it served as a safe house for IRA members on the run from English law. Except for an occasional probe to see if Hawker was interested in helping, O'Neil never talked about the Brotherhood.

And Hawker never asked.

They got together every month or so to play racquetball or spar a few rounds, but even this was becoming more infrequent.

The best friends had taken separate paths. And, as every adult soon realizes, there is no going back.

So all of this went through Hawker's mind as he climbed up the three foot-worn steps and banged on the door. He didn't know how Jimmy O'Neil figured into Saul Beckerman's murder, but he was damn well going to find out.

If O'Neil had somehow gotten on the hit list, he needed to be warned.

And if he had something to do with planning Beckerman's death, Hawker would. . . . Well, he didn't know what he would do.

The porch light blinked on, and Jimmy O'Neil swung open the door, digging a massive fist at the sleep in his eyes.

"This sure as hell better be important—" he began sleepily. But when he saw Hawker, his eyes widened, and his jaw set itself in a wide, craggy grin. "Hawk! What in Mary's name are you doing out and about at this hour?"

"Need to talk to you, Jimmy."

"Problems with the ladies, I suppose?" he said, smiling as he let Hawker in.

"I wish it was something that simple."

Hawker followed him into the kitchen. O'Neil switched on

the overhead light and sat ponderously at the table. "What time is it?" he asked, still confused by sleep.

"Going on two."

"Good God," he said, yawning. "Back in the old days, we'd just now be getting our second wind. Now it's a rare night when I see the clock touch midnight."

Hawker sat down at the table across from him. The years and the miles and the wars had changed Jimmy. It was like seeing old Blair O'Neil all over again. There was the wide, flat Celtic face and the thin, broken nose. The hair was straw-colored, curly and thick except for a slight thinning at the crown. The eyes were a misty gray-green, and they had a sly glint to them. His shoulders were half as wide as the table, and they sloped abruptly over the whiskey-barrel chest, the narrow hips and the knobby, bandy legs that seemed too long and thin to carry O'Neil's two hundred fifty pounds.

Jimmy wore nothing but his sleeping clothes: a pair of blue cotton gym shorts. There was no place to hide the Colt Python .357 he had carried to the door, so he placed it on the table, barrel pointed away from Hawker.

"Expecting trouble?" Hawker asked, nodding toward the handgun.

O'Neil's eyes crinkled good-naturedly. "Expectin' trouble? In Chicago at two in the morning when only lunatics and old friends are out roaming the streets? Ha! Sure, and you're as safe in Chicago as in your own mother's arms."

Hawker chuckled at the sarcasm. "I was thinking of something a little more specific."

O'Neil made a noncommittal gesture. "It's true, I've made an enemy or two in my life. Can you imagine that there was more than one Englishman in Ulster who took an immediate dislike to me, fine human being that I am. Actually threatened violence on my person." He tapped his index finger on the black grip of the Python. "So, I take precautions. Those Orangemen don't give up easily, you know. When they have killing in mind."

"So I've heard," said Hawker.

O'Neil's voice was soft. "I imagine you have. Especially since it was the Orangemen who murdered your mother and two sisters."

"That was a long time ago."

"Forgive and forget, right?"

"I was only four, Jimmy. All I remember of Ireland is green hills and rainy afternoons."

"And the explosion. You remember that. You told me so yourself." He got up suddenly and went to the refrigerator. He popped open two dark bottles of Guinness, and slid one across the table to Hawker. "Hawk, I've never been able to understand why you refuse to acknowledge our cause."

"The Irish cause is your cause, Jimmy. Not mine. There's no doubt that all the misery and suffering the English have heaped on Ireland make it a noble cause. But it's not a reasonable cause. There's no winning that war."

"Only because we refuse to stand as one and fight as one, damn it!" O'Neil snapped. "I'm sick to death of disinterested Irishmen telling me the cause is hopeless when they, themselves, are the reason it is hopeless!"

"I am not an Irishman, Jimmy," Hawker said softly. "I'm an American who happened to be born in Ireland. This is my country now. My cause is here. My fight is here."

O'Neil was silent for a moment, seeming to force his emotions under control. Finally he said, "You're a guest in my home, and my closest friend to boot, and here I am ragging at you about something we've argued about a hundred times before."

It was true. Northern Ireland's fight for independence had been the single point of disagreement during their long friendship. As teenagers, they had fought their one and only fistfight over it; a long, bloody battle that sent each of them wobbling away, neither boy the winner.

Back then, the fight had only brought them closer as friends.

As adults, the old divergence of belief had taken their lives in separate directions.

"You've come to talk," said O'Neil, sipping at his beer. "And judging from the hour, it's something important. I'll not offend you again by goading you away from your business." He grinned. "What's mine is yours, Hawk. Now, how can I help?"

"Information, I guess," said Hawker. He took the crumpled piece of paper from his pocket and pushed it across the table. O'Neil picked it up and held it away to read it, like someone who is farsighted.

He put the paper down. "Who's Saul Beckerman?"

"An acquaintance. He's out of Bridgeport. Maybe ten years older than we are. Short, chubby guy. Made millions in the jewelry business."

"Why is my name on the same piece of paper with his?"

"I don't know. That's why I'm here. Beckerman was murdered tonight. Three guys hit him. Professionals. I got to them about five minutes after they gave Beckerman a flying lesson from a nineteenth-floor balcony."

O'Neil's smile was thin and knowing. "I'd wager the three killers didn't give up this little piece of paper willingly."

"One was an Irishman. I took it off his corpse. The other two didn't sound Irish, but that doesn't mean anything. No I.D.'s on their bodies."

"You killed all three?"

"I didn't have much choice."

O'Neil nodded. "No, I suppose not." He looked at Hawker. "This guy Beckerman—was he Irish?"

"Jewish."

"I don't get the connection."

"Neither do I, Jimmy. That's why I'm here." Hawker hesitated, then put it as plainly as he could. "I want to know if you had him murdered, Jimmy."

O'Neil mused over his beer, toying with the label. "Are you here as a cop, Hawk? Or are you here as a friend?"

"I'm not a cop anymore, Jimmy. You know that."

"Ah, James, James." He smiled. "You'll always be a cop. Don't you think I have some idea of why you took that trip to Florida? Came back with another knife scar—sure, don't think I didn't notice it. And then, jetting off to California like a regular world traveler. You may not be a Chicago cop, but you're still more than just a private citizen, if I miss my guess."

Hawker chuckled. "I'm not going to lie to you, Jimmy. I'm going to tell you the truth because I know I can trust you. I'm no cop. Nothing official, anyway. But when I see things that need to be done, I do them. Another friend of mine supplies the financial backing."

"You've become a bloody private eye!" O'Neil laughed.

"Kind of," said Hawker. "And you still haven't answered me, Jimmy. What's the connection? Did you have something to do with Beckerman's death?"

O'Neil shook his head thoughtfully. "No. I didn't even know Beckerman. But I may know something about his death. In fact, I was thinking of calling you—"

O'Neil stopped in midsentence, cocking his head strangely. He held his index finger to his lips and picked up the Colt Python in his right hand. "I thought I heard something on the porch," he whispered.

"I'll go around the back way," offered Hawker.

"Do you have a weapon?"

Hawker thought about the Colt Commander Chezick had taken from him. "Not with me."

"Some cop you are," O'Neil snickered.

"Give me sixty seconds to get in position. That piece of paper could be a death list. Someone as ugly as you deserves the compensation of a long, full life."

"Hah!" O'Neil whispered. "Ugly, am I? Then it's strange that I still have to carry a stick—just to beat the girls away."

Hawker made his way out the rear door into the city darkness. Wind writhed in the black trees, and there was the sound of distant traffic. September leaves were slick under his feet.

The backyard was enclosed by a chain-link fence—O'Neil's mother had kept springer spaniels before she died—and Hawker stepped over the fence. From the side yard, he could see that his Stingray and O'Neil's old Mercedes were the only cars out front.

It meant nothing. If someone was out to assassinate O'Neil, they would be smart enough to park someplace else and walk.

39

In the darkness, Hawker could see that something slanted against the stone wall of the house. It was a hoe. He picked it up and carried it with him.

There was a rose copse at the edge of the porch. Hawker peered over it. The porch light was still on, and Hawker could see two men. They both wore ragged overcoats and hats.

It took him a moment to place them. Then he remembered: They were the two winos he had seen sleeping on the bench outside Beckerman's apartment.

Only they hadn't been sleeping. And they weren't winos. It was now clear that they had been waiting on the three killers.

Had they followed Hawker? Or was O'Neil on the hit list, and were they simply determined to carry out orders?

Whatever brought them there, Hawker was determined they would not leave until he pounded some information out of them.

One of the "winos" stood at the door. As he tapped lightly at the window, the other wino hugged the wall. In his right hand was a long-barreled revolver.

"Yeah, what do you want?" O'Neil yelled from inside.

"An old friend sent us," answered the wino. "We need to talk to you."

"Who's the old friend?" O'Neil demanded. He was buying time, Hawker knew—time for him to get into position.

"Can't say it out here," countered the wino. "Open the door."

Quietly, Hawker had positioned himself beside the steps. He figured he could jump onto the porch and crack the guy with the gun in the back of the head before he knew what hit him.

Unfortunately, O'Neil decided to move first. Without warning, he punched open the door and grabbed the first wino by the throat. He pulled him roughly into the living room and swung him down onto the floor.

Jamming the barrel of his Python against the guy's head, O'Neil yelled, "I got the bastard, Hawk! It's all clear—"

His words were cut short as the second wino plunged into the room, his revolver snapping off heavy-caliber fire. Before he had time to take firm aim, though, Hawker cracked the hoe handle over his right arm.

The man spun. The shock was plain on his face. Hawker drove his right fist deep into the man's belly. As he hinged forward, whoofing, Hawker used his right elbow to club him solidly behind the neck.

O'Neil lay on his back on the floor. He had been shot in the right hand, and the blood poured freely down his arm. "Watch it, Hawk! He's got my gun!"

Hawker didn't need to be warned. He had seen the first wino dive for O'Neil's Python. He tried to roll away as Hawker's foot hammered at his side. The wino fought his way to one knee and brought the revolver up to fire.

Hawker slapped the gun away with his left hand, and wrestled him to the floor. The "wino" was just over six feet tall and built like a bomb shelter. He muscled his arm under Hawker's shoulder, then clapped both hands behind Hawker's head in a painful half nelson.

Hawker drove backward against him, then used the man's resistance to throw him over his shoulder. The moment he hit the carpeted floor, Hawker was on him. He put all his weight behind an overhead right. The man jerked his head away at the last moment.

It was a fatal mistake.

Hawker had meant to hit the man on the jaw. Instead, his fist crushed the fibrous windpipe beneath his throat.

The man gagged and kicked at the floor, his eyes bulging, hands clawing feverishly at his ruined windpipe.

In less than a minute, the man quivered, still and silent, as the room was filled with the sudden fecal stink of death.

"Christ," whispered Hawker. "I didn't mean to do that."

"The bastards," Jimmy O'Neil raged, holding his bleeding hand. "The stupid son of a bitch deserved to die, Hawk. You did the right thing."

Hawker looked at him evenly. "You don't understand, friend. It's information I wanted. I don't care about him."

"Well," said O'Neil, picking up the Colt Python with his left hand and motioning toward the second wino, "he looks as if he can still carry on a proper conversation."

"It also looks as if we need to get you to a doctor," Hawker said. He took O'Neil's right hand and inspected it. The bullet had torn away the meaty section between O'Neil's thumb and forefinger.

"Will I live?"

"I'm afraid so."

O'Neil chuckled. "It'll take more than these two peckerwoods to kill the likes of you and me. Just like old times, huh? Fighting shoulder to shoulder, kicking royal ass."

"Right," said Hawker.

"Except it was me who usually saved your bacon," O'Neil added with dignity.

"I better get you to a doctor. I think you're going into shock—your memory is beginning to deteriorate."

"Hah!" O'Neil sniffed. "And I'm sure you don't remember the time—"

The sound of the second assassin jumping to his feet drew the attention of both of them. Somehow he had found his revolver during Hawker's fight. He got off one wild shot as Hawker dove for him.

But Jimmy O'Neil's Colt exploded while Hawker was still in midair.

The man was smacked against the porch wall as if he had been hit by a sledgehammer. The impact cracked the front window and shook the floor.

The man collapsed into a heap, eyes wide. Dead.

Hawker lay on his belly on the floor at the feet of the dead man. "Why in hell didn't you just try to wound him?" Hawker demanded. "Neither one of them can talk now."

"And what do you expect?" O'Neil said indignantly. "I had to shoot with my damn left hand. And if you will think back carefully, Mr. James Hawker, you will remember that I'm *right*-handed."

Hawker climbed to his feet. "Well, no use arguing about it." Hawker looked at O'Neil. "I suppose we'll have to call the police."

"Yes, yes, it's our duty," said O'Neil evasively.

"And I suppose your neighbors heard the gunshots. The cops are probably already on their way."

"It's one of the sad things about living in this neighborhood," mused O'Neil. "My neighbors are all so old and deaf, they stop by regularly so that I can listen to their hearts—just to make sure they're still alive."

"I had to blow away those three guys earlier," said Hawker.

"The police commissioner is going to be after my ass for that. When he finds out I was involved in two more killings, he's going to lock me up and throw away the key."

"Hmmmm . . ." O'Neil said thoughtfully. He touched his temple as if he had an idea. "Now, if the two of us were low-life, lawbreaking hoodlums, we'd probably find their car, stuff these two stiffs in, and drive them someplace equally far from our own two lovely homes."

"If we were hoodlums," echoed Hawker.

They exchanged looks and nodded at the same time. "I'll find their car," said Hawker.

"And I'll clean up the mess these nasty buggers have made," said O'Neil.

"I could use a beer afterward," added Hawker. "There's a story you promised to tell me."

"I know a fine little pub called the Ennisfree," said Jimmy O'Neil. "I'll bring the keys."

FIVE

O'Neil drove his old Mercedes, and Hawker drove the death car: a canary yellow rental Chevy, matched to the keys in one of the dead men's pockets.

Who would drive what car was the subject of a short debate. O'Neil was at his gracious, flimflam best.

"You see, Hawk," he reasoned, "if I drive the car with these two dead lads in it, the police stop me, they'll take one look at this mug of mine and figure me for a murderer. Lord knows that's what those nasty Ulster bobbies always thought. May even start shooting before I have a chance to explain—"

"Oh, God—"

"But if *you* drive the death car, Hawk, and the police stop you, they'll just figure you're an off-duty cop doing some moonlighting for our good coroner. You see, it's the kind and honest face you have—"

"Jimmy . . ."

"The face of a young saint, it is, James. Oh, if I could have a face like yours just for a month. Or a week even . . ."

"Jimmy?"

"... there'd be no end to the horrible crimes I'd perpetrate, for I'd be supremely confident that my fine good looks would convince any jury in the land of my childlike innocence. Whoring and drinking—yes, and I'd take a turn at teenage girls, too! And I'm a lawyer, you may remember—"

"Jimmy! I'll drive their goddamn car, if you'll just promise to shut up and let us get at it!"

O'Neil gave him a brotherly pat on the shoulder. "There, now, that's my James, always the first to volunteer for a dirty job."

"I'm beginning to wish that the guy who shot you in the hand had had the foresight to take a gun course. And one more thing, Jimmy. I'm not leaving my car parked outside your house after all that shooting."

"I'll follow you to your apartment then."

"My place is too close, too. And I'll have no alibi if the cops come by or try to call."

"Then where, in Mary's name, do you want to take it?"

"Downtown. Back to Beckerman's apartment, maybe. I can say I was so upset I went for a long walk. It won't take long."

O'Neil shook his head. "You always were prissy about details, James."

Hawker smiled. "I'm still alive, aren't I?"

Twenty minutes later, they had the two corpses propped in the backseat of the canary yellow Chevy. They looked like passengers. Hawker wore gloves, and he had covered the front seat of the car with plastic so he could remove all microscopic traces of his own spore: clothing material, hair, and skin scrapings.

He shifted the Chevy into gear and drove north on

Damen, into the industrial stink beyond the south branch of the Chicago River. The cold September wind was ripe with the foundry and diesel smell of the canal area. Hawker kept his window rolled wide open, because the stink in the car was worse.

It was 3:42 A.M.

The city that never sleeps was asleep.

The streets were deserted. Many of the factories had shut down during the recession. A golden corona of light glowed above the smokestacks of those still in production.

Hawker swung west on Twenty-third Street, sticking to the back streets.

O'Neil followed a safe distance behind.

On Sacramento, Hawker turned south past Harrison High School. A few blocks beyond that, he steered down a deserted alley he knew. He parked the car beyond a garbage bin. He bundled up the plastic and stuffed it far down into the trash.

Even if the police went through the garbage bin for clues, they wouldn't give the sheet of plastic a second thought.

Satisfied that no one was around to see, Hawker slid into the Mercedes beside O'Neil.

"Nice and easy, Jimmy. Get us out of here. Don't drive straight to your bar. Head in the opposite direction. I want to make absolutely sure that no one is following us."

"As good as done, Hawk," O'Neil said softly. And after a long silence, he asked, "Why here?"

"Why what here?"

"Why did you decide to leave the stiffs here?"

They were gliding down Sacramento, through empty streets.

To their left was a hulking civic structure. "I know your sense of humor," explained Hawker.

"What?"

Hawker tapped at the window. "You don't know what that building is?"

O'Neil smiled. The lighted sign out front read MUNICIPAL COMMUNICABLE DISEASE HOSPITAL. "Death is communicable?" he asked.

"Sooner or later, every single one of us catches it," Hawker said soberly. "Some just sooner than others."

When Hawker was satisfied they weren't being followed, he told O'Neil to head for the Ennisfree, the Irish pub he owned on Farrell Street near McGuane Park.

"Fine, fine," said O'Neil. "But first I have to stop and make a telephone call."

"Telephone call? Who do you have to call at this hour?"

"A dear friend of mine is staying at the bar."

"You're turning the place into a hotel?"

"When the occasion calls for it." O'Neil straightened himself behind the wheel. "James, old friend, you've never asked me anything about my dealings with the Irish Republican Army—one of the few Irish-Americans around here who hasn't, I might add. And I've always appreciated it."

"You know how bored I get when you give speeches, O'Neil, I spared myself, not you."

O'Neil ignored the sarcasm. "Even so, it'll probably come as no surprise to you that I've kept my hand in the fight. Right here in America."

"I'm shocked," said Hawker with even more sarcasm.

"Hah! Do you want me to explain things to you or not?"

"I'm listening."

O'Neil nodded. "Chicago and Boston have the largest Irish population outside Ireland itself—you already know that. Most of the Irish in both cities arrived from the home country during or just after the potato famine of the 1840s. An entire nation of subsistence farmers depended on those potatoes to keep their families alive. But during those years, 1845 to 1849, the potatoes caught some cursed blight and rotted before the very eyes of our great grandfathers. Sure, the other crops in the fields were fine. Good grain, fine vegetables. But the English had already stolen our lands, and they demanded the good crops as rent, knowing full well they were sentencing their tenants to death by starvation.

"Yet they still demanded their crops. Starving Irishmen harvested crops grown through their own sweat and saw the food hauled away by English landlords while their own wives and children ate grass. More than a million men, women, and children starved to death during those horrible four years. And the English did nothing. It was genocide; pure and simple, Hawk. They wanted the tenants off the land—land the tenant families had owned and farmed for a thousand years. The knowledge that they stole the land from beneath the corpses of Irish children meant nothing to them, for we have always been less than animals in the eyes of the English."

O'Neil's voice grew husky with emotion as he spoke, and his knuckles were white beneath the heavy bandage on his right hand. "A million simple farmfolk starved, and a million more immigrated to America. The world has forgotten the thievery of the English, and the suffering they caused, but some of those who came to America still remember. They remember that it was the English who banned our religion and made the use of our Gaelic language a crime punishable by death. They remember that the English *still* rule our God-given land, though they have neither the moral or legal right. Thank God they remember, Hawk, for the English have committed a sin against humanity that must never be forgotten."

He looked suddenly at James Hawker. "These are the ones who come to me. They give me money for the Irish Republican Army, and I see that the weaponry the money buys gets to Ireland. And if an Irish-American lad decides he wants to join the fight, I put him in touch with the proper people. And if an IRA soldier must flee Ireland, I arrange for safe passage to this country. You see, Hawk, in the minds of too many, our war over there is an insane fight between Catholics and Protestants. They don't understand the depth of the cause or the righteousness of it. But I swear before God that the war will never end until we have won our country back and freed our lands of bloody English hands."

As O'Neil spoke, Hawker felt the old hatreds move through him, the hatreds he'd thought were long buried. "So you need to call the Ennisfree because you're hiding someone there?" he asked.

"Yes."

"Does the IRA have something to do with Beckerman's murder?"

O'Neil sighed. "Indirectly, I'm afraid. As I said, I had planned to call you, for I need help, Hawk."

"Do you want to tell me about it now?"

O'Neil was quiet for a moment. "After I've made my telephone call," he said finally. "And once I have a glass of good whiskey in my hand."

Jimmy O'Neil found a phone booth on Archer Avenue, then turned southeast on Farrell. The Ennisfree had a red brick facade with canvas awnings and brass door fixtures.

At the door, he knocked three times, slowly. Inside, a single light came on. There was a tumbling of bolts and locks, and the door swung open.

Hawker followed O'Neil inside.

The figure that confronted them in the bar stood in the shadows. O'Neil locked the door behind them, then led the way into a spacious back room.

He touched the lights, and the shadowy figure was revealed.

Hawker was so surprised that he couldn't speak for a moment.

O'Neil's Irish Republican Army fugitive studied his face with a mixture of suspicion and grudging acceptance.

When O'Neil nodded that Hawker was to be trusted, the expression changed to a slow, wry smile.

She was one of the most beautiful women James Hawker had ever seen.

SIX

"Megan Parnell," O'Neil said, smiling, seeing the stunned look on Hawker's face. "I want you to meet my best friend."

Hawker took her hand. It was firm and dry and communicated nothing. "Very pleased to meet you, Mr. Hawker," she said. "Jimmy has already told me a great deal about you." Her alto voice seemed more musical for the Irish accent.

"James," he said. "My father was Mr. Hawker."

She smiled. "Yes, and I've heard about your father, too. And a good Fenian he was, I might add. His last raid on Belfast's Orange Order has become almost legendary."

There was something in the tone of her voice that told Hawker she was chiding him for his own abandonment of the IRA cause.

"My father's dead," he said simply. "Beaten to death by robbers. American robbers."

He closed the topic by turning away from her. Even so, the image of her refused to leave his mind.

Megan Parnell had long, autumn red hair that hung in a

braided rope to the small of her back. Though she was obviously in her late twenties or early thirties, she had the face of a teenage cover girl. The high cheekbones, the bright, demanding blue eyes, the perfect chin that was too wide and firm to be called delicate or even girlish—they all combined to form a truly haunting and unforgettable country beauty.

She wore a plain, gray crew neck sweater over a blue blouse that couldn't disguise the full-busted figure beneath. Her brown corduroys outlined her firm buttocks and her long, graceful legs.

There was a coyness and wit in her eyes that didn't seem to match the seriousness of her attitude or her words.

Hawker looked at O'Neil. O'Neil still wore the sly, knowing grin. He had known the effect Megan Parnell would have on Hawker; indeed, that she certainly had on all men.

Which was exactly why he hadn't warned him that his IRA refugee was a woman.

Hawker ignored O'Neil's smirk. "If you want to fill Megan in about what happened tonight, go ahead. But then you tell me what you know, Jimmy. I've waited long enough."

"Yes, you have," he said, smiling at the woman. "James has the patience of a saint, Megan. It's one of his most endearing qualities." He winked at the woman, then looked at Hawker. "But you know how much better I talk when I've had a bit of something to quench my thirst. My throat is that dry—"

"I'll get it," Hawker interrupted impatiently. "While you talk to Megan. What do you want?"

"A fine Dublin whiskey would be grand. You'll find it behind the bar."

"Where he hides all the good stuff." Megan laughed. "And James, would you be kind enough to bring a tumbler for me?"

"Hah!" roared O'Neil. "Bring the whole damn bottle. This is a night to celebrate, I'm thinking. For my best friend and I will be fighting together once more."

Hawker couldn't help grinning. Though he wouldn't have admitted it to the big Irishman, he felt good about their reunion, too.

Sometimes a man gets tired of fighting alone.

As he walked to the bar, O'Neil threw himself into a detailed story, describing to Megan what had transpired that night. Hawker put the whiskey on a tray with a flagon of soda and a beaker of ice. For himself, he opened a cold Tuborg.

Realizing that it had been one hell of a long night, and that he hadn't eaten in nearly fifteen hours, Hawker searched the kitchen for food. He built a plate of ham and corned beef, rye bread, mayonnaise, brown mustard, and pickles.

By the time he had carried both trays into the back room, O'Neil had finished telling about the assassination of Saul Beckerman and the attack on his own house. Megan was busy removing the bandage from his wounded hand.

Hawker poured two glasses half full of whiskey. "Do you want ice or soda?"

"Heresy!" spouted O'Neil. "Ruin fine Irish whiskey—"

"I'll have ice in mine," interrupted Megan, as if she was used to O'Neil's bluster. She gave him a scolding look. "Now hold your damn big hand still while I disinfect it!"

Hawker sipped at his beer and made sandwiches while the woman did a professional job of cleaning the wound and bandaging it. When she was done, they all ate and drank as O'Neil talked.

"You asked me if I had anything to do with Beckerman's death, Hawk, and I told you 'no,'" he said. "But that's not entirely true. You see, I know who killed him, and I know why they killed him." He swallowed the last of his whiskey, then poured himself another glass before looking at Hawker. "The lads who did it used to work for me."

"Here or in Ireland?"

"In Ireland." He gave the woman a questioning look. "Three years ago, Megan? Or four?"

"Eight, O'Neil—your memory is faulty as usual. You left Ireland three years ago, and that's when they started getting out of hand."

Hawker's boyhood friend nodded. "Eight years ago, James, I arranged for three Irish-American lads from Chicago to join the IRA in Ulster. Their cover story was that they were American students studying in Belfast. We got them jobs, and we put them to work with a fire team. Like most American lads, they were brought along carefully. Sometimes Americans come only for the romance of being able to say they fought the Orange Order. When the work turns boring or deadly, they pack their kits and leave."

"Which happens all too often," Megan interjected.

O'Neil took a chunk of his sandwich, chewing gratefully. "But not with these lads. They came from Chicago, dirt poor and filled with fight. It wasn't long before they were making their own private plans and making independent hits. In an underground army, that sort of thing is sometimes necessary. Even so, they began to get out of hand. It got so they wouldn't check anything through headquarters. I kept a tight rein on them while I was over there, but even so, it was tough going. Once these lads got a taste of blood, there seemed to be no stopping them."

"They became killers, plain and simple," added Megan. "While it may strike you as odd that we in the IRA would disapprove of cold-blooded murder, it's true. We kill quickly and brutally, but we aim to kill only those who actively oppose our cause."

"And the occasional death of a Protestant child is just one of the risks of war," Hawker said coldly.

The remark made her face flush and her nostrils flare. "Forgive me if I don't shed tears over Protestant babies, Mr. Hawker. For you see, eight years ago I scraped the bits of flesh of my own child, yes, and me young husband, too, from the walls of our wee cottage outside Dundalk. I'm sure the ladies of the Orange Order didn't cry for me—but then, the English have had so much more experience at killing, I guess it's to be excused."

"You see, Hawk," O'Neil put in softly. "Megan is from the same east-coast county in Ireland as you. And the Orange Order killed her husband and infant son in almost the exact same way your mother and two sisters were murdered those many years ago."

"Didn't you wonder how I knew about the famous Hulainns of County Louth?" Megan said, still angry and sarcastic. "That was your father's name before he changed it to Hawker, wasn't it? Hulainn? Sure," she went on, "the great Hulainns of Louth. The Fighting Hulainns, supposedly direct descendants of Cuchulain, the great Irish warrior god of Ulster. I've heard the stories about your family since I was just a wee girl on me mother's knee. All about your handsome, dashing father, and how he broke a hundred hearts before marrying, and how his wife and daughters were murdered, and how—before he and his young son, James, escaped to America—his retaliatory strike against Belfast took fifty Protestant lives and began the IRA uprising of 1956."

"If it's an apology you're looking for," Hawker said, locking eyes with her, "I hereby offer it. I spoke out of line. I'm sorry about your family."

Slowly, her face regained its natural color as her anger subsided. She shook her head wearily. "No, it's meself who should be apologizing. I had no right to lay my troubles on your shoulders."

Hawker smiled. "Anytime you need shoulders, mine are available," he said. "I mean that."

"Do you two *mind?*" O'Neil asked, as if offended. "You interrupted me in the middle of my story." He poured himself another drink. "Now I'll have to dampen my throat again."

The three of them laughed, grateful for the comic relief. Hawker couldn't help noticing that, after their short argument, Megan seemed more at ease with him.

There was nothing obvious. He saw it in small things: the way she smiled at him; the way she would reach over and touch his hand to stress a point. She had an electric touch. Hawker couldn't remember when he had felt more physically aware of the beauty of a woman. And, from the unexpected shyness in her eyes, he could see that she felt the sexual tension, too.

So O'Neil told his story—with Megan adding dates and pertinent facts. She had a razor-sharp intellect and an impressive memory for names and figures.

The names of the three Chicagoans who had fought for the IRA were Thomas Galway, Padraic Phelan, and Michael Mac-Donagh. O'Neil said they were a couple of years younger than he was, but Hawker had never met any of them.

The IRA's influence on the three disappeared when O'Neil returned to America. Left without restraint, Galway, Phelan and MacDonagh cut a bloody swath through Ulster.

Their killing became more random, more indiscriminate. Their methods, and the slaughter of innocent victims, began to sicken even veteran Fenians. Whether they were all psychopaths or whether the horror of their first early battles with the IRA had driven them mad, was never clear.

What *was* clear was that they had to be stopped. They had to be driven out of Ireland. And, if that didn't work, it was decided they must be killed.

When confronted, the three Irish-Americans made the reasonable choice. They returned to America.

It was thought that, away from the temptation of killing English Protestants, they would return to normal lives.

"But they didn't," O'Neil explained. "Over a year ago, the three of them resurfaced in Chicago. They made their presence known to me and asked for my help. They were in the process of organizing a terrorist army, an army dedicated to one thing: profit. You see, Hawk, it was their idea to use their experience in terrorism as a business. They would sell Chicago businessmen protection. Protection against criminals. Protection against police. Protection against anything. It didn't matter to them.

"They came to me, pretending some of the profits would go to the IRA." O'Neil snorted. "That's how dumb they thought me to be. I told them their plan disgusted me, and to get the hell out of my bar before I turned them over to the law."

"The three of them went ahead with their plans?" Hawker asked.

"Aye," said Megan. "They did. Unfortunately, they are smart lads. They didn't make their first move until their terrorist army was well organized."

"Right," said O'Neil. "About three months ago, they began to make the rounds of Bridgeport. They talked to every major businessman in the area. They offered complete protection at very high rates. A few of the businessmen went for it right off. The crime rate is high in this area, and I guess they figured safety is worth any price."

"So not many signed up?" questioned Hawker.

"Wrong, Hawk. They almost all signed up. You see, these three lads made it very clear that if their protection wasn't bought, the business owner could be sure he would, in time, lose his business to fire or vandalism—and maybe even lose his life. They intimidate the hell out of people. They dress like a bloody motorcycle gang, and there must be twenty members in their little terrorist army. Irish, black, Italians. Galway, who's the real leader of the three, hired and trained the meanest, roughest men he could find."

"Why in the hell didn't the businessmen go to the police?" Hawker demanded. "Extortion's a crime, you know."

O'Neil nodded. "Of course it is. I'm a lawyer, remember? But you see, Hawk, these lads are local. They know their victims, and individualized terrorism has the greatest impact. The businessmen are completely vulnerable, and they damn well know it. They can be hit at work or at home, through their stores or their families. Hell, if they brought in the police, Bas Gan Sagart could take revenge a dozen different ways."

"Bas Gan Sagart?" Hawker asked. "What the hell does that mean?"

"It's what they call their terrorist group," put in Megan. "It's Gaelic. It means 'Death without the priest.'"

"Death without the priest?" echoed Hawker. "Romantic."

"And all too accurate," said O'Neil. "You've been out of the city for how long?"

Hawker shrugged. "I was in California for a while, then I took a trip up the west coast . . . about two months, I guess. Just got back last week."

"Then you've missed the newspapers. In the last month, there's been a rash of bombings, fires, and shootings in the Bridgeport area. What little resistance Bas Gan Sagart has had been dealt with severely. There will be no more. The businessmen are justly terrified."

"What about the crime watch group my dad and I started?"

"It would be suicide for them to even try to fight back. It would be like a Boy Scout troop trying to fight a team of Green Berets." O'Neil shook his head. "The businessmen in the area are hostages, Hawk. Make no mistake about it. If they don't pay, they're dead men."

"Saul Beckerman didn't pay?"

"That would be my guess. It was a typical Bas Gan Sagart hit: big and messy, for maximum publicity."

"And your name was on tonight's hit list because you've refused to pay."

Jimmy O'Neil made an empty motion of his own confusion. "I trained those three lads. For a year or so, we were as close as four men can be—such is the way with Fenian work. I guess it's a barometer of their madness that they would not make me an exception—not that I would stand for their bullying. Even if they did leave me out of it. But death means nothing to these lads and their little army of killers."

"You could go to the FBI," offered Hawker, and knew the moment he said it exactly why O'Neil could never do so.

"Yes"—O'Neil smiled—"and just explain to the good officers that I'm a respectable IRA gunrunner in need of some assistance? No, Hawk, I'm afraid that's out of the question. I have but two choices. I can either just close down the bar and my law office and just disappear—and fight them undercover, by the methods I know best. Or I can face them head-on and try to destroy Bas Gan Sagart before it destroys me."

"You see, James," said Megan Parnell. "We take care of our own, we do. For good or bad, they're our responsibility. And we must deal with them." Her fists were fixed solidly on her hips, and there was an unexpected coldness in her eyes as she said it.

Hawker paid little attention as O'Neil suddenly rose from his chair and walked quickly toward the bar.

Hawker's eyes were locked on Megan. Once again he felt his stomach stir with stark, physical wanting. "But how can you help?" Hawker insisted, enjoying the way she allowed her eyes to burrow into his. "You're on the run yourself, aren't you? An international fugitive—"

"Who told you such nonsense?" she snapped.

"Well, Jimmy didn't come right out and say it, but that's the impression I got—"

"Utter balderdash. I'm no more on the run than you are"—a light smile crossed her face—"and perhaps even less so."

"Then why *are* you here?"

She looked at Hawker as if he had just asked an inexcusably stupid question. "Why, to kill Galway, Phelan, and MacDonagh, of course."

A moment later, a man's scream for help brought them both to their feet, only to be knocked to the floor by the shock of the explosion that destroyed the Ennisfree. . . .

SEVEN

In that stunned moment, it all came back to Hawker. The deafening, ear-ringing shock of sound. The stink of cordite. The sputtering sound that was burning flesh.

It all came back to him: that time in Ireland . . . that time when he was four . . . that time his mother and sisters died.

But Hawker wasn't a boy now.

Now he could do something about it.

He jumped to his feet and ran toward the main room of the Ennisfree. The entire bar was a roaring flame.

From deep in the flames he could hear a man's screams. He knew it had to be Jimmy O'Neil.

Hawker jerked a tablecloth off a booth and began swinging at the flames, fighting his way toward his best friend. The intense heat seared his face, and he realized the sudden stink was from his own melting hair.

Someone had grabbed him. Someone was pulling him back. It was Megan, her face red and wet with tears.

"No, James, no!" she yelled above the roar of the fire. "There's nothing we can do now. He's lost! He's gone! We've got to get out and save ourselves!"

The screams had disappeared in the din of burning wood and exploding bottles. Megan was holding onto his arm. "Please," she said softly. "We must go now. There's nothing you can do."

Furious, Hawker threw the tablecloth at the fire. "Like hell there's nothing we can do," he said in a cold whisper. He turned to the woman. "Do you have any weapons around here?"

"Well, yes, in the back room where I've been sleeping—"

"Get them," Hawker commanded.

He took one last, long look at the orange flames, which were all that remained of his old friend. The whole front half of the building had been blown away. The door hung broken on its hinges.

Hawker wondered what O'Neil's last thoughts had been. What had he heard that had called him to investigate? A noise? Or just a hunch?

Whatever it was, there was a slight chance the killers from Bas Gan Sagart were still around. Unless it was a time bomb, the explosive device had probably been thrown—or wired to the front door.

And it sure as hell hadn't been there when they first came in.

Hawker pivoted and ran into the back room. Megan was rummaging through a box that was hidden under loose boards in the floor.

"We might as well take everything we can carry," she said, surprisingly calm now. "The police are just going to find this stuff after they put out the fire."

She handed him a pistol-sized Uzi submachine gun. Hawker

checked the forty-round detachable clip, and saw that it was fully loaded with 9mm parabellum cartridges.

As she selected another Uzi for herself, Hawker jammed a Colt M1911A1 automatic in his belt, the military's .45 caliber handgun. From a smaller wooden box marked ROYAL ORD-NANCE FACTORIES/UNITED KINGDOM Hawker took two smooth egg-shaped British hand grenades and clipped them over the back of his belt.

"Let's go," he said. "Move!"

They ran out the back door and into the alley. Megan stopped and looked both ways. "We'll circle the building," she began. "You go that way—"

"Bullshit," snapped Hawker. "You stick right on my shoulder."

"But if you really think they might still be in the area—"

"Damn it, Megan, just shut up and do what I tell you!"

She hesitated, as if she wasn't used to taking orders. "Okay," she said finally. "We'll do it your way, James."

Signaling her to follow, Hawker trotted south down the alley. As they came out onto the main street, a white van screeched around the corner of Farrell. It careened past them.

Hawker got a vague look at a dim face peering at them from the passenger's window. Unexpectedly, the van skidded to a stop, then banged into fast reverse.

"They're trying to run us down!" yelled Megan.

Hawker shoved her roughly onto the sidewalk as the van smacked into a parking meter, just grazing Hawker's thigh. The impact was enough to knock him down.

As he tried to climb to his feet, the passenger door swung open, and a man with shoulder-length red hair jumped out.

There was a long-barreled revolver in his hand, and he cracked off a quick shot before Hawker lifted the Uzi and sprayed him with automatic fire.

The man's head slammed backward against the door as his chest and head spouted blood.

"Behind you, James!" Megan shouted. The back doors of the van had opened, and two men jumped out. Sawed-off shotguns were pressed against their shoulders.

Hawker rolled away from the van, but before he could even raise his weapon, one long burst from Megan's Uzi sent the pair backpedaling into the empty street, jolting and jerking as if they were being electrocuted.

Deciding he no longer had the firepower to deal with Hawker and the auburn-haired woman, the driver of the van popped the vehicle into gear and screeched off.

Megan peppered the back of the van with submachine gun fire as Hawker jumped to his feet. From his belt he grabbed one of the British grenades, pulled the pin, and hurled it overhand as far as he could ahead of the van.

The timing couldn't have been better.

Just as the front wheels of the van roared over the grenade, the grenade exploded. The van bucked upward, then heeled onto its side, skidding down the street until it sheered off a streetlight pole.

Their weapons ready, Hawker and the woman ran after it. Hawker climbed up and pulled open the door. Only the driver remained inside. His eyes were wide and glassy with death. It took Hawker a moment to realize what had killed him. Both of his legs had been shredded off by the grenade.

"Look inside," Hawker commanded the woman. He helped her up so she could see.

"Do you recognize him?"

Megan nodded. "Yes," she said evenly. "It's Michael Mac-Donagh."

"What about the others? Did you recognize them?"

"No. I've never seen them before. They must be part of their terrorist army."

Hawker let the door slam closed and jumped to the asphalt.

The September wind carried the sound of distant sirens.

"We've got to get out of here," he said. "We came in Jimmy's car. I left mine downtown. We'll have to try to hot-wire Jimmy's car."

"No, wait—we don't have to hot-wire it. He used to let me use his Mercedes sometimes. I've got keys," she said, producing them from the pockets of her slacks.

Hawker was already moving toward the front of what was left of the Ennisfree.

Hawker drove southeast on Farrell, then west on Thirty-first Street and down Archer Avenue so Megan would know how to get back to his apartment. Hawker doubled back on Thirty-first, and north on Halsted, toward the Lake Shore Drive penthouse apartment where the long, long evening had begun.

Both hands on the wheel, Hawker rotated his head and neck, trying to work out the knots and tension. Automatically, Megan reached over and began to massage the back of his neck. "I still can't believe Jimmy is . . . is really gone," she said in a small voice.

"They'll pay for it," Hawker whispered. "Each and every one of them, they'll wish they had never been born."

"James, I don't want you to take what I'm about to say the wrong way. I know you and Jimmy were very close. And I don't blame you for wanting revenge. But it's not your fight. You're an American citizen, respected in your community. Hunting down the members of Bas Gan Sagart is going to be a long and bloody job—not to mention dangerous. You see it as revenge. The police will see it as murder."

Hawker almost smiled. She talked as if he was a naive child. But there was, of course, no way she could have known that he had dedicated the last year to busting open networks of organized terrorism.

He had already left a lot of corpses in his wake, none of his killing exactly sanctioned by America's law enforcement agencies. Maybe he would tell her about it one day—but not now.

The only man he had trusted with that information was Jimmy O'Neil.

And O'Neil was dead.

Dead.

There was still a sense of unreality about the word as it traced its way through Hawker's mind, over and over again.

They had grown up together like brothers. They had played together, worked together, and fought together.

But now Jimmy O'Neil, the big, blustering Irishman, was gone.

Dead.

Death had stolen Hawker's whole family. His mother, his sisters, his father . . . and now his best friend. The knowledge that he was totally and completely alone in the world settled on Hawker like a cloud. And now Megan Parnell was telling him to stay out of the fight. To run from the one thing that James Hawker knew better than any other: death.

"I was a cop for a long time, Megan," he said simply. "I know what I'm getting into."

She took her hand from his neck and folded it in her lap. She looked small sitting beside him, with the streetlights flashing by, lighting her face like soft strobe lights as they drove. Hawker felt something akin to pain every time her perfect face was illuminated. It was like no feeling he had ever experienced before.

Maybe it was that silly phenomenon Hawker no longer believed in: love at first sight.

If it wasn't, it was a damn painful facsimile.

"But, James," she insisted. "Wouldn't it be better if the dealings with Bas Gan Sagart were left to someone unknown to the local authorities? Someone who isn't even known to be in this country? Someone who has a whole chain of underground sources to help them, hide them, then aid in their escape when the job is finished."

"Meaning you."

"That's why I was sent here, James. That's what I've prepared for." Her tone grew stern. "For the last eight years, my life has been the Irish Republican Army. When my husband and child were murdered, any normal life I might have had died with them. The cause means everything to me, James. The day *will* come when the Irish rule their own God-given land. And I will not have that grand cause blighted by the likes of these Bas Gan Sagart . . . bastards."

"Then we'll do it together," said Hawker. He reached out and took her hand. "You'll need a place to live, Megan. I want you to stay with me. And when this is over—"

Gently, she pulled her hand away. "Don't," she whispered. "Don't even think of the future, James." She looked at him, her eyes wide and earnest. "I welcome the invitation to stay at your apartment. But you must promise me something."

"Sure, Megan—"

"You must promise that we will live there as . . . as team-mates. Or friends, if you feel me worthy of your friendship. But never as lovers, James. You must not hurt either of us by think-ing of me as your future lover."

For a moment, Hawker didn't know what to say. It was as if she had read his mind. "We hardly know each other," he started, "and I wouldn't think of expecting—"

"Never, James," she insisted. "You must never think of me that way." She reached over and began to massage the back of his neck again. "And please don't think it's because I can't care for you, for I already do. And I think I could come to care for you more than you could ever know."

"But why, Megan?"

She touched her finger to his lips. "Please, James. Just prom-ise me."

Hawker turned off Lake Shore Drive into the parking lot of the late Saul Beckerman's apartment building. He said nothing. He pulled in behind his Stingray and left the Mercedes running. He got out, closed the door, and leaned into the window.

"You'll find a key to my apartment in the mailbox, Megan. There's food in the refrigerator and clean sheets on the bed. My landlady's name is Mrs. Hudson. She's Scottish, and you'll love her. In the morning, she can help you get fixed up with fresh clothes and whatever else you might need."

Before he turned away, Hawker kissed her tenderly on the forehead. He could see that her eyes were moist. "Whatever problems you have, Megan, we can work out together," he said. "But I can't promise what you ask. I'd only be lying to you. And to myself."

"Then tell yourself the lie," she whispered. "Because what you want can never be. . . ."

EIGHT

There was a note on the windshield of Hawker's Stingray. He read the note, then checked his watch.

It was 5:20 A.M.

The morning delivery trucks were already gearing down the empty streets, preparing for a new day.

He read the note again. It was from Felicia Beckerman.

James, please stop by the apartment. Please. I don't care what time it is. It's impossible to sleep, and I dearly need to be with someone. We can have a drink.

Hawker tried to think of all the excuses he could give her later. Tell her he'd never gotten the note; maybe it had blown off his windshield. Tell her he had had a friend pick up his car. Or tell her the truth: that he was suddenly disgusted with women in particular, and life in general.

It's not every night you hear the dying screams of a boyhood friend.

And it's not every night that you are scorned by a beautiful woman before your attentions are even offered.

We can have a drink.

Hawker crumpled the note and banged it off the wall of the apartment building.

He could use a drink.

The front doors of the building were locked, so Hawker pushed the little button over Saul Beckerman's brass nameplate.

He was surprised at how quickly the lock immediately buzzed open. Felicia hadn't been lying when she said she couldn't sleep.

She was standing in the doorway, waiting for him. She wore a long, filmy, turquoise nightgown. Her dark hair had been combed down over her shoulders. In the dim light of the hallway, her Italian complexion appeared even darker, her lips fuller, the silhouette of her heavy breasts and the shadow of hips more mysterious.

"I'm so glad you came," she whispered, kissing him lightly on the cheek.

"You said no matter how late—and it's almost daylight, you know."

She took his arm and led him to the couch where the negress and the businessman had been performing. She sat close beside him, as if cold or frightened.

"I know exactly what time it is," she said, her voice as weary as her eyes looked. "I knew at one o'clock and at two o'clock, and every minute and every hour afterward."

"I thought the doctor was going to give you something."

She laughed sadly. "After a night like tonight, it would have taken a club to put me out." She was silent for a moment, then touched Hawker's arm. "It was awfully kind of you to come, James."

Hawker stood quickly and crossed the room to the bar. "I'm not feeling very kindly, Felicia. In fact, I'm feeling just the opposite. Drink?"

He poured a shot of brandy for her, then measured half a glass of Scotch for himself. He reconsidered for a moment, then filled his glass the rest of the way. He drank it down in three burning gulps, then poured himself another.

He heard Felicia get off the couch, heard her cross the room, and felt her touch the back of his neck. He wondered how there could be so much difference in the touch of two women.

Megan's touch was like electricity, cool and clean, a shock to the heart.

Felicia's hands were warm and wanting but filled with loneliness, like the drawings of winter trees in her bedroom.

"You *are* upset, aren't you?" she whispered.

"Yes," he said. "Yes. I guess I am."

"Is it because of Saul? Because you had to kill those men?"

Hawker turned and placed the glass of brandy in her hand. "Yes," he lied. "That's the reason."

Her dark eyes burned into his as she put the brandy to her lips. "I've been sitting here hating myself all night, James."

"Hating yourself? Why?"

"Because . . . because I'm glad Saul is gone. Not murdered the way he was. He wasn't a good man, but he was a kind man. And I wouldn't wish anything so horrible on him. But I'm glad in a sick, sick way, because it has freed me. And I've been hating myself because I know how wrong it is to feel the way I do."

Hawker gulped his second drink and poured himself a third. "What do you want me to tell you, Felicia? That it's okay? That what you feel now is normal and natural, and that you shouldn't feel guilty about it? Do you want me to play the kindly man-friend with the soft shoulder again? Well, damn it, Felicia, I'm not in the mood. And what you're feeling *isn't* natural, for Christ's sake. Your husband has been murdered, woman. And you should have the goddamn decency to at least *act* like you're sorry."

His words smacked into her like a hammer. He watched every word hit its mark, banging away inside the delicate head. She seemed to draw into herself, trembling.

"I'm sorry," Hawker said quickly.

She pulled away from him. "No," she said. "No. You're right. It's true. I *am* awful. God, what a beast I am!"

She buried her face in her hands, her whole body convulsing. Hawker took her by the shoulders and turned her gently to him. He led her to the couch and sat down, holding her.

The sobs seemed to originate at the very roots of her being. The horror and sadness and guilt came pouring out.

Hawker almost envied her. For the first time in a very, very long while, he, too, felt like crying.

He held her, saying nothing. Every time he thought the tears had finally subsided, her face crinkled anew, and a fresh wave of anguish swept through her.

But, inevitably, it ended, and she leaned against him as limp as a rag doll. Hawker pushed her gently away and returned with a box of tissues. She scrubbed at her eyes and blew her nose. "God," she whispered. "What a display."

"I'm sorry, Felicia. I was damn cruel."

"Oh, James, you weren't cruel. You were just being honest. And the truth is exactly what I needed. It broke the emotional doors down. A good cry, that's what I needed. Your honesty did what Saul's death or the doctor's drugs couldn't do." She took a deep, fresh breath and blew her nose again.

"I guess I'll be going then."

She grabbed his arm as he stood. "You helped me, James. I'd like to help you."

Hawker's expression was wooden. "I'm not sure that's possible," he said.

Felicia stood and wrapped her arms around him, her face on his chest. Hawker noticed that she was trembling, trembling as if she were freezing. She whispered, "Sometimes life can be so . . . so shitty, it would be nice to be able to just disappear for a while. Not forever. Just an hour. Or a day. Someplace to escape to where no one or no memory could find you."

Hawker stroked her soft hair. "Yeah," he said. "That would be nice."

"On a night like tonight?" she asked.

"Especially tonight." He pulled her tighter. "God, woman, your skin is like ice."

Her eyes were as wide and wet as a fawn's. "It's because I'm lonely, James. And I want to escape. With you. Tonight."

She stepped back, and in one motion stripped the nightgown over her head and dropped it on the floor. Her nipples were full and brown on her heavy breasts. The undulation of her ribs veed into a narrow waist and the black slash of pubic hair. "Tonight, let's pretend there is no one else and nothing else but you and me in the world. Please."

Hawker pulled her close to him, his mind scanning for the right words of refusal.

They swayed together, back and forth, in a slow, soundless dance, and soon he stopped fighting for words.

Her hands moved tenderly on Hawker's body. She found the buttons on his shirt, and soon her breasts were like hot coals against his bare chest.

"You're so tense," she whispered, massaging the back of his neck. "I'm going to help you relax, James."

Hawker said nothing as his hands slid over her cool hips.

Her lips had found his ear, and her tongue was warm and smooth. "We're going to escape together," she whispered. "I'll do anything you want me to do, James, absolutely anything for your pleasure. Tonight we're people without names and without memories."

Her hot tongue dampened Hawker's lips, then traced its way down his chest to his abdomen. Felicia's hands slid down Hawker's ribs as she dropped to her knees. He heard the clank of his brass buckle coming undone, and then she pulled his pants down, finding him and holding him in her small hand.

"I've been wanting to see you like this, James," she murmured as she rubbed her cheek against him, kittenlike. "I know it's wicked of me, but I just don't care anymore."

She kissed the inside of his thighs as she massaged his testicles. And then she opened her mouth and slid her lips over him, taking him deep inside her, the suction of it seeming to pull at his very soul.

Hawker found the soft weight of her breast with his right hand, toying with the projectile shape of her nipple as his left hand tangled her hair and formed a fist.

She took him softly at first but then became increasingly demanding, attacking him in her passion; the two of them finding the ageless, sliding rhythm of the mind's one escape beyond death.

Felicia stopped for a moment, and her words came in staccato gasps, as if she herself were approaching climax just through giving. Her fingers were buried deeply into Hawker's tight buttocks as she whispered, "You're so strong, James, so quiet; you hold too much inside, don't you?"

Hawker came very close to smiling. "Keep that up for a few minutes more, and you'll find out just how right you are."

Her eyes were like a cat's. "Then I will," she purred. "And when the time comes, don't warn me. I want all of you. As much as you have to give. . . ."

NINE

Hawker awoke with a start and checked his Seiko diver's watch.

It was 9:14 A.M.

He had been asleep for just over an hour.

Felicia slept beside him in the massive round bed. The sheet was pulled up only to her stomach, and her breasts were rounded and flattened by their own weight. Her black hair was spread like a fan over the pillow, and her face looked prettier and younger in repose.

Hawker realized that it was the first time he had ever seen her that she looked at peace with herself.

Holding himself on one elbow, he leaned over and kissed the dry lips. In her sleep, she whispered, "More, please . . . more . . ."

Smiling, Hawker arose and found his clothes. He dressed quickly and found paper and pen.

He wrote:

Back to the world, Felicia.

*   *   *

He didn't sign it.

Outside, Chicago was loud with the business of making business. Hawker drove carefully, keeping pace with the lunatic traffic. He pulled over at a sidewalk Cubano restaurant and purchased a *café con leche* from a very small man with a very big cigar.

The coffee was rich and sweet, and he sipped it as he drove.

At the old sandblasted graystone where he lived, Hawker parked and trotted up the steps. For the first time, he thought about Megan Parnell.

Jimmy O'Neil's Mercedes was nowhere to be seen, and Hawker was glad that she had been shrewd enough to hide it in the little garage.

There was no doubting her intelligence. Or her toughness. Why couldn't the IRA have found the same qualities in some hatchet-faced, bovine woman—or better yet, man?

Why did they have to send this woman? This woman whose haunting beauty and fiery blue eyes left Hawker to search the validity of his own immediate wanting.

What in the hell was it about her?

He knew that if he had to sit down and draw his ideal woman, it would be Megan Parnell. The way she smiled; the wry glint in her eyes; the musical rhythm of her words.

After his divorce, Hawker had vowed never to get emotionally involved with a woman again.

And, aside from a few minor transgressions, he had kept the promise. To Hawker, women were to be used and then left behind.

Until Megan Parnell came along. But because of some strange loyalty to a dead, young husband, she had made it damn plain that his attentions—or the attentions of any man—weren't welcome.

She had entombed herself in the nunnery of the Irish Republican Army cause.

Why? So she could die like Jimmy O'Neil and twenty-five generations of other freedom-loving Irishmen?

It all seemed like such a damned waste to Hawker. And, as he opened the front door, he decided he would do his best to convince her that she was traveling a long and lonely road, a road without victory or even thanks at the end.

The decision cheered him. Megan could turn him down but not before he had had his say.

Hawker's landlady, the widow Hudson, was making breakfast noises in the kitchen. Mrs. Hudson was a doughy, apple-cheeked woman with a Scottish brogue and a grandmother's instincts.

Because she had no children of her own, she seemed to take special delight in mothering him and clucking over him.

Hawker tolerated it because he liked her and because she didn't insist on doing all the little domestic duties that Hawker preferred to take care of by himself.

Except for the cooking. He let her handle the cooking, and twice a day when he was in town, she carried an excellent breakfast or supper on a tray upstairs, the whole of which was Hawker's apartment.

Also, she had never been the least bit inquisitive about his professional life. And, in Hawker's business, that was important.

His romantic life, though, was another story. She worried over the rapid exchange of women in his life. Secretaries, teachers, nurses, doctors, actresses, and singers. Hawker could go a month without seeing a woman. But when the mood was on him, the traffic into his Archer Avenue apartment was brisk.

Hawker strode into the kitchen and gave her an exaggerated slap on the rump. Her face showed mock outrage underlined by pleasure.

"Well, 'tis about time you came crawlin' home, Mr. James Hawker, with your face looking as much like that of a tomcat as it does your own."

"Ha!" Hawker sniffed the air experimentally. "Are those bran muffins I smell?"

"They are," she scolded. "And you'll not be touching a one until you've had a proper breakfast—and a shower. You look like you've been wrestling with half the hussies in Bridgeport."

"Only half?"

She turned the lengths of bratwurst sizzling on the stove and shook a fork at him. "It's an outrage, if you be askin' me, Lieutenant Hawker—not that it's any of my business."

"'*Lieutenant*' is it?"

"Yes. Out all night with God knows what sleeping on the pillow beside you; drinking hard liquor, if I'm to be trusting my nose. Which I do. And that nice young Megan Parnell upstairs crying her dear eyes out this morning, waiting for you. Why I should concern myself, I don't know—"

"Ah?"

"Yes, and her a fine and proper lady if I've ever seen one." Mrs. Hudson smacked the fork down on the counter and drew

82

a deep breath. "Far be it from me to intrude in your private life, Lieutenant. If you want to end up a lonely old bachelor, it's your business. But you're of the age to be siring fine-looking man-children, and, if you choose to waste your seed on common floozies instead, it's none of my business. . . ."

Hawker was smiling. "It isn't?"

"No!" She wagged her finger at him. "But I saw the look in the eyes of that lovely young Megan when she came looking for you this morning, and I know that look, Mr. James Hawker. She cares for you, she does. Wandered in here like a lost little kitten—"

"We just met last night." Hawker laughed.

"As if time makes any difference! I'd only known my own sweet Charlie—God rest his soul—five minutes, and I knew he was the man for me." She set about piling bratwurst and poached eggs, toast, coffee, and cream on a tray, then placed it on the kitchen table. "Now you carry breakfast up to that sweet young thing and apologize properly to her." She planted her fists on her hips. "Not that it's any of my concern, but to my way of thinking, Lieutenant Hawker, you've kept her waitin' like a . . . like a—well, I'll *say* it!—like a common whore!"

Hawker put his arm around the old woman and hugged her to him. "Such language, Mrs. Hudson!"

She blushed and sputtered. "Well, I'm mad, I am."

"I can see that."

She patted his arm affectionately. "The wee lass cares for you, James. I've seen many a lovely young woman climb those stairs but none that hold a candle to her. You must treat her better."

"I'd love to. But I'm afraid you have it all backward, Mrs. Hudson. Megan told me we can't be anything but friends." Hawker winked at the widow. "Go to work on her. Tell her what a great guy I am, would you?"

She sniffed. "Well, I try not to make a habit of prying into your affairs—"

"Oh, I know that. I know that."

She winked back at him. "Well, maybe just this once." A smile lit her handsome Scottish face. "But I have a feeling she already knows the kind of man you are."

Hawker carried the tray up the stairs. He tapped on the door, then pushed it open with his foot.

In the small living room, the only sign of her presence was her clothes, neatly folded over Hawker's leather reading chair.

From the bedroom, a voice called, "Is that you, Mrs. Hudson?"

"No. But I'm carrying the breakfast she made for you."

"James!" In a moment, she appeared in the bedroom doorway. She wore his high school football jersey as a nightgown, and she had tucked a blanket around her hips, saronglike. The delight in her face changed immediately to disapproval. "I've been worried about you!"

The morning light that came through the window brought out all the color of her blue eyes and the autumn subtleties of her hip-length auburn hair.

Hawker placed the tray on the table. "I didn't want any arguments about who was going to sleep in my bed. You needed sleep, so I decided to stay with a friend."

Hawker hoped she would ask if his friend was a woman, then immediately cursed himself for thinking like a high school kid. It didn't matter, for she didn't ask.

"I could eat a horse," she said, eyeing the breakfast. "James, would you be kind enough to toss me my clothes?" She made a helpless motion. "I'm not to be trustin' this blanket I'm wearing."

Hawker shook his head as he got them. "I'm getting tired of all these tough decisions you make me wrestle with."

She smiled as she returned to the bedroom. "You're a dear, James. Thank you."

In a moment, she returned wearing the same blue blouse, sweater, and corduroy slacks she had worn during the long night before. Hawker watched as she tore into the breakfast, enjoying the childlike abandon with which she ate.

Megan stopped suddenly, a chunk of toast protruding from her mouth. "Aren't you going to be eating?"

"I don't know. Mrs. Hudson is pretty mad at me."

"Mad? But why?"

"She thinks I've treated you badly. She says that you're a 'true lady' if she's ever seen one, and she thinks it's scandalous that I made you wait in my apartment alone."

Megan chewed the toast down, sly humor shining in her eyes. "She's an intelligent woman, that one."

"Does that mean you agree?"

She laughed and flipped her hair. "It means whatever you care to make of it." Megan grew suddenly serious. "Are you feeling better, James? I really was worried about you. About what you might do."

Hawker poured himself a cup of coffee from the ceramic pot. "After I left you last night? After I left you, I let myself be seduced by a widow. Weird," he said, "but I'm suddenly surrounded by women who have lost their men. Mrs. Hudson. You. And my recent bed partner."

"Don't be cruel, James. We have no time for it. I'm glad you found someone to take your mind off things. It can help a man. I know."

Hawker gulped his coffee. "Oh? I'm surprised. You really do have a good memory, don't you?"

Instead of looking offended, she smiled, which irritated Hawker even more. She stood and kissed him lightly on the cheek, then began gathering her empty dishes. "I'm sorry if I hurt you with what I said before we parted this morning, James. It's something you can't understand. Not now. Someday, perhaps. But not now."

Hawker caught her wrist as she reached for the empty rasher. "Maybe I understand better than you know, Megan," he said, startled by the intensity of his own voice. Even so, he held her wrist and went on. "I understand that you're a woman. A beautiful, healthy woman at what should be the prime of her life. But instead of allowing yourself to follow your own natural destiny, you've decided to tie yourself to a hopeless cause. And I'll tell you something else, Megan. It's going to wither you. It's going to dry you till you're like a badly stretched skin. Sacrificing all of your natural wants and needs and desires because you suffered a personal disaster eight years ago—"

She snapped her wrist away. Hawker expected her to be angry. He hoped she would be angry, angry enough to discuss her feelings with him.

But instead, she lifted her eyes toward his in a long, slow look of pain. Hawker felt the look in her eyes cut like a laser right through to his heart. He wished there was some way he could wash all of the pain from her, all of the hurt and horror that her life had brought her. He wished there was some way he could shoulder it himself; some way to wrestle the demons away from her so that she could be light and free and filled with fun—the way Hawker knew she had been, once.

He tried to tell her what he felt, but the words wouldn't come. Instead, all he could summon was a mumbled "I'm sorry, Megan."

He made a show of studying his watch and yawning. "I'm going to get some sleep. I'm going to need it."

"*We're* going to need it," she corrected.

"Okay," he said. "We're going to need rest. Because tonight we go to work."

She looked surprised. "We're going to attack Bas Gan Sagart already?"

Hawker shook his head as he walked toward the bedroom. "The preliminaries, Megan. I'm a thorough man. The preliminaries first. They take time. But they can keep you alive."

TEN

Hawker awoke ravenous.

He hadn't eaten breakfast, and he had slept through lunch.

Megan had left him a note:

I've got to do a bit of shopping. A woman needs more
than one change of clothes.

Hawker smiled at the Elizabethan swirls of her penmanship.
Even her damn handwriting was pretty.

He showered the sleep away and did the rugged list of calisthenics he should have done that morning but didn't. Seventy-five slow push-ups. A hundred sit-ups with a twenty-pound weight, cold on his chest. Stretching. Then thirty fast pull-ups on the wooden bar mounted in the corner of his room.

Then he pulled on nylon shorts, a sweat shirt, and Nikes. As he trotted down the steps, Mrs. Hudson's voice called out, "Will you be back in time for a proper supper?"

"I will! Make double orders of everything. I'm starved!"

"And no wonder," he heard her retort. "What with being out all night and sleeping away the good part of the day. . . ."

Hawker was out the door before she finished.

He jogged down Archer, then south on Kedzie. He started slow as his leg muscles stretched and lubricated themselves. Then he picked up speed, running at a steady seven-minute-mile pace.

At Marquette Park, he cut across the golf course. In the brisk September air was the sweet smell of crushed grass beneath his feet. The leaves on the oaks and maples had turned to the warm colors of a Florida sunset.

Or Megan Parnell's hair.

He pushed the thoughts of her from his mind by concentrating on business. The business of life and death.

He knew very little about the pseudo-IRA terrorist organization, Bas Gan Sagart. He had to find out more before he could even set the groundwork for his assault.

Maybe Megan could add a few pieces to the puzzle. After all, she had supposedly been on their trail for the last month.

He would ask her. He would set her down and pick every bit of information she had out of her—with no more talk about love and future hopes.

It had been stupid to begin with. The more he thought about it, the sillier he felt.

He now lived the kind of life he wanted to live. He was aloof and alone. Free to come and go as he damn well pleased.

He had no woman to worry about or cater to. When he wanted to travel, he traveled. When he wanted to eat, he ate. As a bachelor, he lived his life without worry or guilt.

So why in the hell would he want to change that?

Hawker hacked and spit as the sweat beaded and began to pour down his face.

He wouldn't—didn't—want to change, damn it. Women were to be used and left behind.

And Megan Parnell was just one more woman. If she wanted to live like a nun, that was her business.

There were other women. Plenty of them.

And if Megan got in his way on this job, or slowed him down, he would tell her to get the hell out and go back to Ireland, to her precious cause.

Feeling better for the lies he'd told himself, Hawker circled back on Fifty-fifth Street as passenger jets, like aluminum frigates, rumbled over Midway Airport. With less than a mile to go, Hawker opened his stride, arms plunging in perfect rhythm as he powered home.

Above all other things, this was clear: Bas Gan Sagart had murdered Saul Beckerman, a man who'd probably wanted to hire Hawker for protection. Worse, they had murdered Jimmy O'Neil, the closest thing to a family member Hawker had left.

And now they would suffer for it.

As he sprinted toward Archer, Hawker vowed that they would pay—each and every one of them.

And the last thing they would hear before they drew their final breath would be Hawker's voice.

Megan hadn't returned by supper, so Hawker ate alone, pretending he wasn't disappointed.

When he was done, he returned to his room and called Jacob Montgomery Hayes.

Hayes was both a friend and a business associate.

After Hawker had resigned from the Chicago Police Department because of all the bullshit bureaucracy, Hayes had summoned him to his museumlike lakeside estate in Kenilworth.

It was Hayes's idea that Hawker, who had more than proven himself as a brilliant and merciless terrorist fighter, still had a job to do. All across America, Hayes had reasoned, there were hardworking men sickened by the crime and fear in their own neighborhoods. They wanted to fight back but didn't really know how.

Hayes made Hawker a proposition. If he would agree to become a vigilante, Hayes—America's third richest man—would finance everything.

And Hawker had agreed.

The teaming of Hayes's money and connections with Hawker's firepower had already mounted two successful assaults: one in Florida; the second in Los Angeles.

Now, before he took on Bas Gan Sagart in Chicago, Hawker wanted to tell Hayes of his plans.

Hawker didn't need Hayes's blessings to act. But he might need his help.

Hayes's acid-witted butler, Hendricks, answered the telephone. Hendricks had worked in British intelligence during the war, and Hawker was beginning to realize that the old Englishman served as more than just a manservant around the Hayes estate.

Hawker had a suspicion that much of the tactical information Hayes gave to him actually came from some of Hendrick's old intelligence methods—or even sources.

"Hendricks, old buddy," Hawker said into the phone. "It's me!"

"How pleasant," said the cold, formal voice. "But I'm afraid we don't know any 'me' here, sir, so, if you don't mind we shall hang up."

"Come on, Hendricks." Hawker laughed. "It's James."

"Yes. The manners should have told me as much."

Hawker's voice grew serious. "I need to talk to Jacob. Can he come to the phone?"

"He's in his study tying bits of hair to a hook, I'm afraid. Deadly serious business."

"And you can't interrupt him? It's important."

"Of course we can interrupt him, sir. But we prefer you come in person." Hendricks hesitated, then added, "The telephone is such a public instrument, you understand."

Hawker was surprised by the implications. Someone had bugged the phone of one of America's richest men?

"I'll be right out, Hendricks."

"We shall be waiting on tenterhooks, sir."

Hawker wrote a note to Megan telling her to wait until he got home, then caught the expressway to Kenilworth.

Hayes's mansion was built of native rock, and set deep within a rolling park of trees at the edge of Lake Michigan. It looked more like a museum than a house. The entire estate was encircled by a high black wrought iron fence.

At the gate, the electronic surveillance system studied him for a moment, and then the gates swung open. Hawker drove slowly down the winding, asphalt drive. There was the nutlike odor of fallen leaves, and the wind carried the smell of wood smoke across the lake.

Hendricks greeted him at the door. He wore a flawless black tuxedo, and Hawker realized that he had never seen him dressed any other way.

"Mr. Hayes is waiting for you, sir," he said.

"What was that business about the phone, Hank?" Hawker asked as he followed him down the marble hallway. "Does someone have a phone tap on?"

"We will let Mr. Hayes tell you, sir."

"But you're the one who worked in intelligence, Hank."

The butler's eyebrows raised slightly. "Is that so? Yes. We had almost forgotten." Hendricks knocked and opened the study door, announcing Hawker's name as if he were entering a formal ballroom.

Jacob Montgomery Hayes looked up from his fly-tying vise and smiled. He was a chunky, balding man in his early sixties. He wore gold wire-rimmed glasses, and there was a briarwood pipe clenched between his teeth. His clothes all looked like they came right out of an L. L. Bean catalogue. Khaki slacks. Pendleton wool shirt. Vibram-soled walking shoes.

"Going on another fishing trip, Jacob?" Hawker asked as they shook hands.

"James," he said warmly. "It's good to see you—and convenient, too."

"Oh?"

Hayes waved Hawker into a leather chair beside the fireplace, then sat down across from him. "Yes, it's convenient because I was going to send you a message tonight, anyway."

It was one of Hayes's idiosyncrasies. He never called. He always sent a messenger, as if it were the 1890s and the telephone was just a passing fancy.

"What about?" Hawker asked.

Hayes smiled and shook his head. "No, we'll save that for later. You've come to see me, and Hendricks said it was important. How can I help, James?"

Hawker shrugged. "I'm not sure you can. There's a small terrorist organization operating in Chicago, and I'm going to hit them. It's my problem, and I think I can handle it. But since you are the closest thing I have to an employer—as well as being a friend—I thought you should know about it."

Hawker grinned, trying to make light of what he said next. "Besides, you never know—these guys might get lucky and put me out of commission before the job is done. If that happens, someone should know what's going on. It would take the police a year to run them down legally, and another year to put them away. But, if I fail, the next logical step is to let the authorities know about it. And someone needs to know enough about this terrorist group to talk sensibly to the police."

Hayes nodded and lighted his pipe. "I see. By all means, tell me about it. It sounds serious."

So Hawker told him about Beckerman and O'Neil, and about Bas Gan Sagart. Leaving out his own emotional involvement, he even told Hayes about how the Irish Republican Army had sent Megan Parnell after the three renegades.

As Hawker talked, he noticed Hayes grow increasingly interested. He no longer toyed with his pipe, or the deer-hair streamer he had been attaching to a hook. He sat hunched toward Hawker, listening intently, asking only for an occasional clarification about something he didn't understand.

When Hawker had finished, Hayes restuffed his pipe with tobacco from the walnut humidor on his broad desk. He lighted the pipe and exhaled smoke that smelled of maple trees. "Your story interests me more than you might think," he said. "And I assure you, if there's any way I can help, I will. We will treat it as a joint venture. All of my resources are at your disposal. I will assign Hendricks to get whatever information he can on these people"—his smile was thin and knowing—"not that you require much help when it comes to collecting important data. In fact, on this particular campaign, your sources may be better than ours, and you certainly have more mobility."

Hawker nodded. "Hendricks didn't say it, but I got the impression someone had a tap on your telephone. Is that why you suddenly lack mobility?"

Hayes looked amused. "Until you stopped by, I didn't know why I lacked mobility. Now it's suddenly very clear to me."

"I don't follow you, Jacob. What do you mean? Does it have something to do with why you wanted to see me?"

Without answering him, Hayes pulled open a desk drawer and handed Hawker a neatly folded note. It was written in plain, block letters to disguise the handwriting. Hawker read it, shocked.

"They came to the chairman of my corporation," Hayes explained. "They wanted to see me, but I'm necessarily hard to reach—on a business basis, anyway. When the chairman passed on news of their visit to me, I saw it for what it was: an attempt at extortion thinly disguised as a business offer. We refused them, of course. Hendricks found the note tacked to the front door today. How they got through the security system, not to mention the attack dogs which roam the grounds at night, I'll never know. That's why I wanted to see you, James. I wanted to see if you had any ideas on how to deal with these people."

"I have plenty of ideas on how to deal with them," Hawker said between clenched teeth as he read the note for a second time:

Chicago can be a dangerous place for a rich man. No fence can keep out a murderer. You should reconsider our offer. Bas Gan Sagart.

ELEVEN

That night, Hawker carried the same weapons he had taken from the secret cache in the back room of the Ennisfree.

The Colt military .45 was a good weight in the holster on his belt. The Uzi submachine gun, freshly oiled and armed, was behind the seat. From his own small arsenal, he had added two AM-M14 TH3 incendiary hand grenades.

Hawker wore a black Aran Island sweater to keep out the cold, and a black wool watch cap.

Megan Parnell rode beside him, surprisingly calm considering they were about to break into Bas Gan Sagart's heavily armed headquarters. He had warned her more than once that, if they were caught, the chances were slim of them having enough firepower to fight their way out.

Not if Bas Gan Sagart's twenty-man army happened to stumble on them, they wouldn't.

She had acted like she hadn't heard the warning. "I still think it's too early to attack them," she had said flatly.

"We're not attacking them, damn it, Megan," Hawker argued.

"I just want to get into their headquarters and plant some eavesdropping devices. Hell, I hope we don't have to fire a single shot. Not tonight, anyway. But we need more information. We need to know the specifics about Thomas Galway and Padraic Phelan, the two leaders. Where do they live, by what routes do they travel? And I'd like to hear how their men talk when the two leaders aren't around. If the men aren't happy with Galway and Phelan, Bas Gan Sagart should be an easy nut to crack."

"It doesn't matter if they're happy," Megan insisted. "They're all getting rich. That's all they care about—money. And they'll fight to the death for it."

Hawker had to force himself not to reply. She had a way of infuriating him, and the most infuriating thing of all was, he knew he reacted to her barbs all out of proportion to their intent because he was falling more deeply in love with her.

But more than that, he owed her a great debt.

During her month in Chicago, she had done a professional job of gathering information on the terrorist group. Without drawing any attention to herself, she had uncovered a wealth of valuable data.

She had found out several names and addresses of group members. She had compiled a list of twenty-five businessmen who had been pressured into making payoffs. She had connected four murders and seven fire bombings directly to Bas Gan Sagart.

But the prize of all her work was locating the group's headquarters: a grim, abandoned factory building off Joliet Road on the polluted Des Plaines River.

The one thing she hadn't been able to discover was where

the two leaders, Galway and Phelan, lived. She had tried every-thing, she said, including covering almost every likely street in Chicago by car or on foot.

Their residence remained a mystery.

Hawker couldn't fault her initiative. But that didn't make their relationship any less antagonistic—on Hawker's part, anyway. For Megan seemed to refuse to allow herself to be tricked into any meeting of emotions. Aside from a few tender looks Hawker caught her giving him (her eyes darted away the moment she realized he was observing her), she remained pro-fessionally aloof.

Hawker drove in silence. He turned north on Ninety-sixth Avenue, and followed it over the river. The sooty foundry lights reflected dully off the water, as the smokestacks spouted smog.

They rode in Jimmy O'Neil's Mercedes. Hawker had care-fully dabbed the license plates with mud so they were unread-able.

There wasn't much chance the police would be looking for O'Neil's car—not this soon, anyway.

But Hawker didn't want to take any chances.

The Bas Gan Sagart headquarters was part of a short chain of deserted steel mills, the corpses of big city industry.

The factories loomed over the narrow side street like can-yon walls. In the sweep of headlights, Hawker could see there had been a feeble effort to board the doors. NO TRESPASSING signs had been posted, then partially ripped away by vandals. The windows had been broken out on the first two floors of most of the buildings.

"It's that one," Megan said, pointing toward the last building in the line. It was set apart from the others, looking like some gigantic abandoned car on its lot of weeds, raw earth, and rusted junk.

"You've been past it before?"

Hawker could see her face in the green glow of the dash-board lights. She nodded. "Twice."

"In this car?"

"And would I be letting you drive by it again if I had?" She indulged in a private smile. "I'm not dumb, James. Each time, I hired a taxi. The drivers both thought I was quite mad. I had them driving all over this part of Chicago, pretending to be looking for the house of a long-lost relative whose address I'd lost."

Hawker chuckled. "I've got to stop second-guessing you, Megan. I'm beginning to think you know more about this business than I do."

"Do you mean you doubted it?" she asked wryly.

Hawker drove past the abandoned factory, noting there was one dim light burning on the second floor. He circled back on Joliet and backed the Mercedes into a quick-sell car lot on a side street.

"When we walk back to the factory, just act like you own the city," Hawker said to her as he locked the car. "Nothing draws attention faster than someone trying to look innocuous."

"I think I can handle that."

"And if a squad car patrols past us, press the Uzi against your hip, so it blends in with your legs as you walk. And if the squad car slows, pretend like we're—"

"Really, James," she sputtered, "I've been through this sort of thing before."

"Oh?"

"Yes. And I'm beginning to resent your—"

At that very moment, a police car idled around the block on patrol. Just before its lights swept across them, Hawker grabbed Megan by the shoulders and pulled her roughly to him. He held her in a long, soft kiss until the car had passed by. For a moment—a brief, brief moment—the kiss became real as Megan began to react, her lips growing hot and moist.

When he released her, she exhaled deeply. "My, oh, my," she said.

"I was about to say pretend we were lovers."

"The demonstration was adequate."

"I think you could be a pretty good kisser, if you'd just let yourself go for a moment. Honestly, Megan, you're so tight most of the time, a blacksmith couldn't drive a pin up your ass with a hammer."

"Is that sort of talk really necessary?" she said primly as they walked on.

"I just don't understand you, that's all."

Her voice became even and businesslike. "You don't have to understand me, James. And I don't have to understand you. All we have to do is find a way to destroy Bas Gan Sagart."

"Ah. I keep forgetting. You're a soldier."

"That is correct."

"In that case, *soldier*, get behind me. And keep that weapon lower."

She obeyed without comment.

They made their way straight to banks of the Des Plaines River, then followed it west to the factory.

The riverbanks were littered with trash and abandoned junk. There was an acid stink to the water. Beyond the darkness of the river was the eerie glow of downtown Chicago; a sulphur yellow glow, like fire through a fog.

The grounds of the factory were encircled by a chain-link fence topped with barbed wire. One corner of the fence had been beaten halfway down by neighborhood kids, and Hawker helped Megan over it.

He pressed his hand against her ear and whispered, "They might have a guard out. Or a dog. Be ready."

She nodded and followed him toward the back of the building.

Hawker tested a massive set of double doors, probably built so the factory could take on ore from river barges.

They were locked, as were the two other back doors.

"We could blow the locks," Megan suggested in a whisper.

"Blow the locks? Why don't we just call them and tell them we're coming? No, we'll have to crawl through a window."

The windows were about seven feet off the ground. Hawker searched until he found one almost completely broken out. He took off his sweater and wrapped it around his hands, then jumped up and pulled himself through. He dropped down onto the cement floor of the factory's interior. When he was sure there were no guards around, he opened a side door for Megan.

Hawker took out a small Tekna pocket flashlight and twisted the cap until the bulb flared on. "You stay just behind my right shoulder," Hawker whispered. "Keep your weapon ready."

She nodded and walked after him through the darkness.

Most of the machinery had been removed from the factory,

so it was like walking through some massive, deserted gymnasium—except for the stink of foundry dust.

There seemed to be no signs of recent occupation, and Hawker began to wonder if it really was the rallying place for the terrorist army of Bas Gan Sagart.

Maybe Megan was wrong.

He decided to have a thorough look around before saying anything to her. After all, she hadn't been wrong yet.

Hawker made his way across the center of the steel mill. The small flashlight panned back and forth, showing inoperative machinery. Some of the machinery was covered with tarps.

In the far corner of the room were the dim shapes of more tarps. But something about the shapes was different. Hawker lifted a chunk of canvas and searched underneath with his light.

Car tires. He lifted the tarp higher and saw the side of a white van—the same kind of van they had destroyed.

Megan's sharp intake of breath told him that she, too, had made the association.

There were three more vans beneath tarps.

Hawker checked the doors. They were locked.

"They must meet upstairs," Hawker whispered.

She nodded. "There was a wee, dim light on as we went past."

"I know. Keep your weapon ready."

Along the west wall was a heavy freight elevator. Hawker followed the edge of the wall until he found a set of steel stairs.

He lifted his Uzi submachine gun and slowly made his way up the steps.

At the top of the stairs was a steel fire door. Hawker knew that if it was locked, their mission would have been in vain. He would have to be satisfied with bugging the ground floor—and, from the looks of things, that wouldn't produce much.

Carefully, he lifted the big lever that sealed the door. It caught, then gave way.

Hawker exhaled with relief as he swung the door open just wide enough for them to get through.

The second floor comprised a wide hall that seemed to open into three main rooms. A weak light showed through the doorway of the room on the north side of the building.

Hawker held up his hand. Megan stopped behind him as they both strained to listen.

From the room came the blurred rumble of men's voices. There was the occasional gust of soft laughter, followed by an increase in voice volume. Only then could Hawker hear well enough to understand what they were saying.

Two words stood out above all others.

It was a name. A name that made Hawker's hand grow tight on the submachine gun.

Jimmy O'Neil.

Apparently, they found his horrible death humorous. The name was followed by more laughter.

Death by fire, Hawker thought grimly. He vowed then and there that many of them now laughing would live just long enough to experience the horror of such a death.

The other two massive rooms were dark. With Megan following him, Hawker made his way into each of them.

The first room appeared to be a combination office and

kitchen. There were desks, a stove, two long tables, and some chairs.

There were telephones on each desk. Hawker didn't expect their numbers to be printed on the dials, and they weren't.

He unscrewed the transmitter cap off each phone as Megan held the light. Using a tiny screwdriver, Hawker connected the red, green, and yellow wires to the candy-colored listening devices he had brought.

He replaced the transmitter caps and put the phones back as he had found them.

From his pocket he took three single-sensory transmitters. They were the size of a quarter, nearly flat. He stripped the adhesive open at the base of the bugs and put one beneath each desk, and the third beneath the table where they ate.

Finally, he tested the file cabinet doors.

As he expected, they were locked.

Hawker made a motion for the woman to follow and peered out into the hall. He could still hear the faint conversation from the lighted room.

They slid down the hall and ducked into the next opening.

The second room was a type of dormitory. Hawker guessed it had been the worker's shower room when the factory was still in operation.

Bunks lined two walls. Only a couple of them were made. More blankets were stacked in the corner.

Hawker took two more of the single-sensory bugs. He hid one beneath the water closet of the toilet. He had just placed the other beneath a table in the middle of the room when Megan suddenly grabbed his shoulder.

"Listen!" she whispered.

At first, he didn't know what she was talking about. But then he heard them, too.

Footsteps.

Footsteps coming their way.

Both of them moved quickly across the room and pressed themselves against the wall beside the door. Hawker could feel the barrel of the Uzi, cold against his cheek.

The footsteps came progressively closer. The man was humming to himself. A quick, Latin tune.

Hawker hoped the man would walk right on past them into the lounge area. He hoped their good luck would continue to hold.

It didn't.

TWELVE

Still humming, the man came into the dormitory and flicked the switch on the wall.

When the lights came on, he was standing face-to-face with Hawker. Hawker saw his face contort with shock and surprise. It was a thin, feral face: black greasy hair; sly, mean eyes; skin pocked with acne.

The man jumped back to yell. Hawker reached to grab him, but before he did, Megan brought the knife edge of her right hand down on the back of the man's neck.

It didn't knock him out. But it shocked him just long enough for Hawker to spin him around in a hammerlock and clap his hand over the man's mouth.

Hawker's voice was a harsh whisper as he spoke into the man's ear. "Make so much as a sound and I'll rip your goddamn arm off and shove it down your throat. Got it?"

The man nodded quickly.

"Good. Just walk and keep quiet. We're getting out of here, and you're going with us."

He motioned for Megan to lead the way.

Hawker kept the man's arm pressed tight against the middle of his back. He seemed resigned to the fact that he had no chance of escape. It soon became obvious that that's exactly what he'd wanted Hawker to think.

Halfway to the steps, just as they passed the freight elevator shaft, the man suddenly dropped to his knees, spinning down and under, freeing himself from the hammerlock.

Surprised, Hawker stumbled over him and almost fell. The man put all his weight behind an uppercut that hit Hawker flush in the scrotum. Hawker wheezed and buckled to the floor, feeling the pain move through him like red heat. Sweat beaded on his forehead.

Somehow, a knife materialized in the man's hand. Hawker managed to roll away just as the man dove at him. The blade of the knife clanked hard against the steel floor.

Using her submachine gun like a club, Megan swung down at the man's face. He smacked the weapon out of her hands and grabbed her by the blouse, trying to jerk her down onto the blade of the knife.

Her shirt ripped open as buttons scattered across the floor. It freed her of the man's grip—and saved her life.

It also gave Hawker just enough time to fight his way to his feet.

He kicked the knife out of the man's hand, then clubbed his jaw closed with a sizzling right. The man *whoofed* with pain as he slid backward across the floor.

Hawker was immediately on him. He dragged him to his feet. The man hit him twice in the temple with a weak right hand. Hawker ignored it. He buried a left into the man's stomach, then knocked his throat crooked with a smashing right fist.

The man backpedaled toward the second-floor wall. But he never hit.

For a microsecond, Hawker couldn't figure it out. The man seemed to disappear before his eyes.

But then he heard the gagging scream, and he knew.

The elevator shaft. He had fallen down the elevator shaft.

"Let's get out of here," Hawker whispered hoarsely.

There were shouts behind them as they ran down the stairs. Hawker led the way, gun poised coolly in his right hand.

"If we can just get outside, we've got it made," Hawker yelled to Megan. "The only thing between us and the car is a door."

Hawker learned all too quickly how wrong he was.

As they got to the base of the stairs and headed through the cavernous darkness of the factory, the front doors of the building opened with an electronic hum. A moment later, a van came wheeling through.

The headlights of the van swept the building's interior, catching Hawker and Megan in midstride. The van immediately jolted to a halt, and men spilled out. From the corner of his eye, Hawker could see more men coming after them, down the steps.

"Take cover!" he yelled to Megan. "We're going to have to make a fighting retreat."

As they dove behind a gigantic steel press, Hawker noticed absently that the woman's blouse was still open. In the stark white light of the van, her breasts appeared marblelike; full and firm beneath the sharp cones of her nipples.

Gunfire began to ricochet around them. Hawker dropped to his belly, and the Uzi rattled like a spinning chain, hot in his hands.

Two men coming from the second floor grabbed at their ruined faces and fell over the railing to the cement below. A man who had been standing behind the door of the van suddenly dropped to the ground, writhing in agony. Hawker realized that Megan had been firing, too.

Hawker yelled "Hey!" to get her attention, then made a leap-frog motion with his hand toward the back of the factory. "And we've got to make it quick—before they realize what we're doing. You'll go first."

She nodded. "Just say when."

Hawker rolled out, spraying the men with automatic weapon fire. When he had them pinned down, he yelled, "Now!"

Immediately, Megan sprinted toward the rear of the factory. When she had found cover, Hawker punched in his only fresh clip for the Uzi and ducked away from the curtain of fire which screamed through the mill.

Most of the fire was coming from behind the van. But the Bas Gan Sagart men were beginning to spread out, trying to circle them. Hawker knew he had to waste a bunch of them at once, if they were to have any hope of escape.

He could see Megan's face from where he sat crouched behind the steel press. Her expression was grim but calm. She gave him a questioning look. When Hawker had readied himself, he nodded. Immediately, she began spraying the van with 9mm slugs. When the Bas Gan Sagart men ducked, Hawker stood to his full height and pulled the pin of an incendiary grenade. He gave it a full two-count before he hurled it overhand at the van.

There was a minisecond of silence between the rapid-fire volleys of Megan's Uzi. The moment was punctuated by a scream of fear as the grenade rolled under the van, and the men on the other side saw it.

Then there was a deafening explosion, and a brief corona of smoke and light billowed above the fresh stink of burned flesh.

Two men came tumbling out from behind the van. Their clothes burned on them in a bright white blaze. Their screams were terrible to hear.

The incendiary grenade Hawker had thrown was filled with 750 grams of thermate, or TH3. For nearly a minute, the thermate would burn at a withering 2,150 degrees Celsius.

There were more screams behind the van. The screams quickly turned to moans as the thermate seared their flesh—and then their lives—away.

As Hawker sprinted to cover behind Megan's position, he wondered absently if the burning men had been the ones he had heard laughing about Jimmy O'Neil's own death by fire.

He hoped so.

As he raced past Megan, she lifted her submachine gun as if to shoot him. Hawker ducked forward as her weapon spouted fire. Immediately to his right, one of the Bas Gan Sagart soldiers who had been sneaking up to ambush him gagged and jolted backward as his heart pumped blood through the holes in his chest.

Hawker was about to nod his thanks to her, but the movement of two dim figures at the rear of the building drew his attention.

As a head appeared over a dark clump of machinery, Hawker immediately dropped to his stomach and opened fire. A chunk of the head was catapulted backward.

The dead man dropped to the ground without a sound.

Hawker waited and watched. He had seen two men, not one.

Megan was drawing more fire behind him now. He wondered how long she could hold out. If she could just give him time to secure the area at the rear of the factory, they'd have a fair chance of making it out. It would be a race, but, for once, the odds would be in their favor.

Hawker began to crawl toward the clump of machinery where the dead man lay. Amazingly, one of the headlights of the van still burned through the haze of smoke that enveloped the building. The intense heat of the grenade had radiated throughout. That, combined with the stink and the low moans of the dying, made it seem all too much like a man-made hell.

Grimly, Hawker vowed he would not die here, not with a woman as spectacular as Megan Parnell at his side.

There was a bullet waiting for him. Someplace. Sometime. That he well knew.

But not here. Not like this. And not before he had had his time with Megan.

He still couldn't figure out where the second man had hidden. It was as if he had disappeared.

Hawker crawled around the machinery. The ruined head of the man he had just shot was a seeping, dark blob an arm's length away from him.

Hawker gave a final look around, then decided to stand.

Just as he got to one knee, something hit him from above. The impact was so great that, for a timeless moment, he thought he had been shot.

But then he realized it was the second man. He had been hiding on top of the machine and had jumped Hawker as he passed beneath.

The collision knocked Hawker to the ground, and his Uzi went flying. He struggled to his feet, then froze as the man jammed the barrel of a thick automatic in his face. He heard the hammer click back.

The man was breathing heavily. "You're a dead man, motherfucker," he wheezed.

Hawker held a small metal ring out to him. "If I'm dead, you're dead, asshole," he said easily.

"What's . . . what's that?"

Hawker held out his second and last thermate grenade. The fuse cover was held on only by his index finger. "It's the pin to this. If I go, you go, too."

The man's laughter was forced and nervous. "You ain't got the balls, buddy."

Hawker smiled and let the fuse cover fall to the ground. "That's where you're wrong—*buddy.*"

"Hey, you're . . . you're fucking nuts!" The man took two frenzied strides and dove for cover. Hawker whirled and threw the grenade at the back wall of the building. It banged off the cement foundation and exploded in a brilliant white light, blowing an opening in the wall.

In one smooth motion, Hawker drew the military Colt .45

and drilled two slugs into the man as he lifted his head to see if Hawker had been blown up by the grenade.

"Megan!" he yelled. "Now!"

She sprinted toward the gaping hole in the wall as Hawker's .45 pounded off covering fire.

When the clip was empty, he ran after her, the two of them fleeing into the fresh night air and the cover of darkness, sprinting for their lives and away from the hell they had helped create. . . .

The few Bas Gan Sagart members who pursued them turned back when they discovered that both Hawker and the woman could shoot on the run.

The terrorists obviously didn't like fighting when the odds weren't heavily stacked in their favor.

Hawker didn't indulge in back-street routes now. He took the shortest way possible back to the Mercedes. It seemed to take forever, but they finally made it to the car lot. Hawker unlocked the door for Megan and, with a quick glance over his shoulder, jumped behind the wheel and squealed out into the empty street.

It was 2:12 A.M.

Megan was breathing heavily. He noticed that her hands shook as she hid the Uzi on the floor behind them.

"Do you happen to have a cigarette on you?" she asked.

"I don't smoke."

"Neither do I. But I think I'd make an exception tonight." She began to feel under the seat, hunting for something.

"What are you after?"

She smiled suddenly and held up a pint bottle. "This. Dear Jimmy always kept a wee touch hidden away—for hot days and emergencies, you see."

"I'd call this an emergency," Hawker agreed. Megan took a long draw from the bottle, then handed it to Hawker.

He let the whiskey slide hotly down his throat, then gave the bottle back to her. "You all right?" he asked.

"While we were fighting, I was too busy to be scared. I'm making up for it now."

"The next time you tell me it's too early to do something, I'm afraid I'll have to listen."

She shook her head emphatically. "No," she said. "You were right. We had to take the chance. I should have done it before, but I was . . . afraid."

"Can't blame you," said Hawker. "Did you recognize any of those guys?"

"I saw Thomas Galway and maybe Phelan, too. I think they were among those who came running down the stairs after us. But they took pretty good cover the moment we started firing. I didn't see them again."

"No chance of their being dead?"

"No. That would be nice to think, that we had ended it all with one fell swoop. But I'm afraid not. They stayed behind cover the whole time. Like the cowardly murderers they are, they left the fighting and the dying to their men."

Hawker's hands grew white on the steering wheel. "Next time," he whispered. "Next time we'll get them."

"Right now, all I want to do is have a shower and get into some . . . different clothes."

He watched her as she tried to hold her torn blouse together with one hand. Even so, Hawker could see the heavy rise of her breasts. He made no secret of the fact that he was looking.

Her face colored. "What about you?" she asked. "Are you all right? That fellow hit you pretty hard."

Hawker cringed just thinking about the shot he had taken between the legs. "I may need a long soak in a warm bath—and my voice may be an octave or two higher—but I'll live."

She chuckled and seemed to relax for the first time. "I'm glad." She smiled. "I'd hate to see half the pretty young ladies in Chicago forced into mourning."

Hawker reached out and pulled her toward him. She fought him for a moment, then let her head rest against his shoulder. "I don't care about the pretty young ladies in Chicago," he said. "I care about you."

She pulled away from him. "Don't, James. Please."

Hawker touched her face tenderly. "I'm going to tell you something, Megan. I'm going to say it because I have to say it. But once I've said it, I'll never say it again unless you ask me to. I love you, Megan. From the very first moment I saw you, I've loved you. I know I'm talking like some passion-crazed school-boy, but I can't help it. There's something about you, Megan . . . it's like I've known you all my life. You feel it, too. You may not admit it, but it's true. I can see it in your eyes."

She sighed and was quiet for a time. "Yes, dear James," she said finally. "It is true. And I feel it perhaps even more strongly than you do."

"Then why in the hell can't you just let go, Megan? To hell with Bas Gan Sagart; we ruined them tonight, even if we didn't get Galway and Phelan. And to hell with my work and your IRA." Hawker looked straight ahead, eyes frozen on the road as he spoke, almost as if talking to himself. "I'm sick of the smell of death, Megan. And I'm sick of hopeless causes. Sure, the world needs its fighters. Too many people are running scared. But we've done more than our share."

He reached out and took her hand. "Mrs. Hudson told me I should be raising a family, and she's right. But I've never really felt ready until I met you, Megan. We have the chance to make something good of our lives. It's not too late, you know. We could leave all this behind and go someplace; someplace where we could make a fresh start. Florida, maybe. Or southern Ireland, if you like." He squeezed her hand and released it. "Think it over, Megan. We'd make some awfully beautiful babies."

She sniffed, and Hawker realized that she was crying. "It can never be, James," she said softly. "But I will think about it—I promise. When both Phelan and Galway are dead."

"Are they so damn important?" Hawker demanded fiercely.

"They are to me, James. When they learned the IRA wanted them out of Ireland, their last act of violence was against my own family."

"You?"

"It was me they were after, but I wasn't there—and God curse me for being away. They made do with my sixteen-year-old sister. They raped her, James. They attacked her like animals. Galway, Phelan, and MacDonagh. And I can't rest until they pay for their terrible deed."

THIRTEEN

The two of them spent the next two days resting. Megan had a liking for long walks through the city. She said the color of the leaves reminded her of autumn in Ireland.

Sometimes Hawker would jog along beside her. But more often, she insisted on going alone. She always returned brighter and happier than before, her face glowing as if enjoying some private joke.

They were cordial—even affectionate—but in the fashion of old friends. She was at her best when they submerged themselves in long rambling conversations over tea at night.

It was only then, it seemed, that they could put all the tension of their mission, and the awkwardness caused by Hawker's proposal, behind them.

Hawker was both surprised and pleased by the number of similar interests they had. After the death of her son and husband, Megan had enrolled in Trinity College in Dublin, majoring in biology. Hawker had majored in law enforcement, but biology was his minor. And, like Megan, he had a student's interest in natural history.

They were both fond of chess. They both disliked playing cards. They both loved old movies, but neither of them liked television. Their tastes were similar in dozens of other instances. And it didn't stop there. More than once, they would both turn and begin to say exactly the same thing at the exact same time, then laugh uproariously.

The more he came to know about her, the more confident Hawker was that she was as close as he would ever come to finding his perfect mate. And he was even more determined to convince her of it.

But he promised himself not to broach the subject again. If she wanted to talk about it, she would have to bring it up.

And he knew that would never happen until Thomas Galway and Padraic Phelan were dead. He didn't blame her. Hawker understood her grim determination to destroy Bas Gan Sagart.

It was more than just the mad fixation of someone possessed by a political cause.

It was a personal quest. The destruction of Phelan and Galway was a mission of personal honor.

Once when she was out, Hawker spent an hour making phone calls.

He called Felicia Beckerman to see how she was getting along. She sounded subdued but clearly happy to hear Hawker's voice. Felicia had just gotten back from the funeral. Her emotions seemed to ride a roller coaster even as they talked.

Their evening together had been a delight, she said. The rabbi had been curt to her at the funeral. She was thinking about leaving Chicago, maybe take a world cruise—would Hawker like to come? There had been more questioning by the police concerning Saul's death. How long had she known Hawker? Had she ever seen before the three men Hawker had killed? Was Saul involved in anything illegal? She was anxious to see Hawker again, she said. Her nerves were shot, and she could use another night of escape.

Hawker hung up, surprised to find that he liked Felicia better than he had previously thought. Beneath the stylish, jet-set exterior was a simple woman who wasn't afraid to communicate honest emotions.

His second call was to Jacob Montgomery Hayes. Hendricks answered, as he'd expected. Hawker questioned him about the new security measures he had suggested. No, there had been no more notes tacked to the door. Yes, there was one new development: Bas Gan Sagart had been in touch with Hayes's corporate headquarters by telephone. They wanted to describe their protection program to Hayes personally. They wanted to tell him just how valuable it might prove to be. They said they would give him a few days to think about it before calling back. No, they refused to give a return number.

Finally, Hawker tried to reach Inspector Boone Chezick at police headquarters. He wasn't in, so he leafed through the Chicago phone book until he found his home number.

Chezick answered on the second ring.

"Boone? It's James Hawker."

"Oh, yeah, the famous trigger-happy ex-cop, right?" Chezick needled.

"You know what the great thing about not being a cop is, Chezick? I can punch just about any smart ass's lights out, and not worry about losing my *bars.*"

"Jesus, Hawk. I was just kidding." Chezick forced a thin chuckle. "Something I can help you with?"

"I was wondering how the follow-up on the Beckerman murder was going."

"Well, your story checks out, if that's what you mean. The paperwork boys will be calling you downtown soon to take a statement, and you may even have to talk to the D.A. But you got nothing to worry about. Like I said, your story checks."

"And what about the guys who wasted Beckerman?"

"Aside from being real dead, you mean? Well, I've had a hell of a time getting a line on them."

"Does that mean you found out something?"

Chezick immediately became suspicious. "Why's it so important to you?"

"Just nosy, Chezick. I've been reading stuff in the papers that bothers me. There's been a lot of killing going on lately."

"Tell me about it, Hawker," he snorted. "It's like a fuckin' war zone around here lately. And something very big went down two nights ago we ain't even releasing to the news boys 'cause it might start a goddamn general panic."

"So why don't you fill me in, Boone? My curiosity's been working overtime."

"It wouldn't have something to do with that mick's bar getting firebombed, would it?"

"That 'mick' was Jimmy O'Neil, Lieutenant. And he just happened to be my best friend."

"O'Neil, huh? That's who we figured it was. The damn body was burned so bad—" Chezick had the good manners to catch himself. "Anyway, until the lab gives us the official word, we've been working on the assumption that it was O'Neil. And O'Neil was involved in that IRA shit."

"You think there might be a connection?" Hawker tested.

Chezick became cautious again. "You're Irish. You tell me."

"For Christ's sake, Boone. If I knew something about it, wouldn't I have found a way to help O'Neil?"

"Maybe you did find a way, Hawk. There was a vanload of guys blown away outside the Ennisfree the night of the bombing."

"Come on, Chezick. You know I don't give a shit about politics. And that includes Irish politics."

The big Polish cop thought for a moment, then said, "Yeah, I guess that's true, Hawk." He laughed. "I must be getting a little paranoid. Anyway, I think there's a connection. I think a few of your Irish cousins are trying to organize themselves into a big-time crime network, and it stinks clear through. They're trying to shake money loose from some very big people, and—" Chezick caught himself again. "And that's all I'm going to tell you, Hawk. Sorry."

"But you haven't found them yet?"

"Hawk, if they live on land, we can track them. If we can track them, we can find them. And I'm not saying another word about it."

So Hawker made small talk for a time, trying to dig a few more facts out of Chezick. When Chezick refused to be tricked, the two of them laughed together at Hawker's craftiness, and he wished Chezick luck before saying good-bye.

It was a hollow wish.

Hawker's one great fear now was that Chezick would get to Galway and Phelan before he did.

Sometimes, when Megan didn't know he was watching, Hawker would study her perfect face, the auburn hair, and the sleek lines and curves of her body, trying to memorize everything about her.

There was an air of nobility about her—in appearance and in mind. And Hawker knew she couldn't allow herself to think about the future until her quest had been fulfilled.

So he went to work.

The listening devices he had planted in the Bas Gan Sagart headquarters had been found, of course. In fact, Hawker's Tobias Seismic Recording system had monitored the entire search. On tape, Hawker had the sound of the candy-colored transmitting devices being crunched.

But the tape made it possible for him to hear Galway's voice—as identified by Megan—for the very first time.

It was a little higher than he'd thought it would be, with an oily smoothness. Galway retained just a touch of accent from his years in Ireland. And that's all they got from their night of bugging.

But he still had his computer. Hawker was no electronic wizard, but he had grudgingly come to the conclusion that it was the computer age. He could either sit back and scoff—and suffer from his own ignorance—or he could jump to the head of the line and see what computers had to offer.

He chose to jump to the head of the line, and he'd never been sorry. His 128K RAM terminal had been invaluable in more than one criminal case.

So now he put his computer to work on two names. Thomas Galway. And Padraic Phelan.

While Megan slept in his bed, he worked far into the night at his computer, using the RUSTLED software programmed by a brilliant and occasionally crooked friend of his. The software program made it possible to pirate any computer in the city.

First, he checked the license number he had noted on one of Bas Gan Sagart's vans.

Galway and Phelan obviously liked irony, for the vans were registered to a fictional corporation at the same address as the Ennisfree.

He could picture the two smirking at the thought of the police checking the same Department of Motor Vehicle file after the bar had burned.

Hawker checked references and cross-references in every other government data bank he could think of. The public records on Phelan and Galway were easy to follow up until the year they left for Ireland. But slowly and surely, Hawker was getting a mental picture of the two men he now hunted.

And it wasn't a very pretty picture.

As teenagers, they had spent their lives in and out of trouble. Fights. Drunken brawls. A stabbing. They were suspects in the murder and robbery of a Kenilworth elderly couple. Both were charged in a multiple rape case, but the charges were dropped when the victim refused to testify against them.

Jimmy O'Neil had described them as "tough and full of fight."

But they were more than that, Hawker was learning. They were vicious. They liked to kill. And they liked to be in control.

Megan had described Galway as the leader, a linebacker-sized hood with long red hair, sloping shoulders, and a face like a boiled ham. She said he had a funny way of laughing. A high, sharp intake of breath, like a wheeze. He was the planner, she said. The brains. He was the one who had dreams of being rich.

Phelan, she said, was an overweight scarecrow with bad skin. A coward—and, like all cowards, vicious when the scales were tipped safely in his favor. Everything about him was sharp angles and rolls of fat. A tall, awkward, gawking man out of the Lincoln mold, but without the Lincoln grace. In the IRA, he became known as a back-shooter. And there were rumors he liked to disfigure victims after he had killed them.

The more Hawker learned about them, the more he wondered why Jimmy O'Neil had recruited them. Obviously, they had lied to him about their past. But hadn't he even done some preliminary checking on them? Perhaps he had. Perhaps he was desperate. Desperation is, after all, the hallmark of all hopeless causes.

The computer gave him facts and figures and histories. But it wasn't enough. He had to know where to intercept them, where to find them. The chances of their going back to the headquarters were slim. Their little terrorist army would be in disarray. They would be on the run. And it was a possibility, as

Hawker had to admit to himself, that they may have already left Chicago.

But his instincts told him different. His instincts told him they were still around. Like all small-time crooks with dreams of grandeur, they would try to bleed their scam of one last big score.

And that's when it hit Hawker. Suddenly, he knew where to intercept them.

He knew their next logical move.

And he could only hope that America's third richest man wouldn't mind being used as bait.

FOURTEEN

It was 3 A.M.

Hawker sat cramped in a stand of trees, hidden away in a blind of oak limbs and leaves, ten feet above the ground.

Before him, the ribbon of Sheridan Road veered away north and south into darkness, a cold ribbon of gray in the white glow of a quarter moon.

Behind him, the solitary lights of Jacob Montgomery Hayes's mansion glimmered through the September trees. A wind moved off the lake, cold in experimental gusts, as if testing itself for winter.

The dark trees clattered and writhed in the darkness, alive with the wind.

Hawker waited.

He waited just as he had waited the night before. And the night before that. And the night before that.

And each night, he saw nothing. He heard nothing. And he grew increasingly concerned that maybe—just maybe—his instincts were wrong.

Perhaps his premature hit on Bas Gan Sagart's headquarters had spooked Galway and Phelan.

And perhaps they had correctly seen Jacob Montgomery Hayes's profane refusal to their final extortion offer for what it was: a challenge.

Because that's just what it was. When they called his corporate office only three days earlier to see if Hayes would see them personally, one of Hayes's trusted officers had given them his message. And he had given it to them word for word: *If the bastards want me so bad, tell them to come and get me.*

It was a challenge, all right.

But it was also a trap, and Hawker was now afraid that Galway and Phelan were smart enough to suspect it.

Even so, Hawker waited.

Over the past three nights, he had added pillows and blankets until the deer stand in which he sat was fairly comfortable.

He wore the thick black, oiled-wool sweater. The black watch cap was pulled down over his red hair.

A blanket was pulled over his legs to keep out the wind. Across the blanket lay a Colt Commando Rifle. The Colt fired 5.56mm ammo at a cyclical rate of close to 800 rounds per minute.

Atop the automatic weapon, he had mounted a Star-Tron Mark 303a night-vision scope. The scope was about the size of a good camera, but it was a hell of a lot more complicated. It worked on the principle of light intensification. The objective lens collected all available light: starlight, moonlight, even the dim light from Hayes's mansion. The objective lens then focused the light into an intensifier tube, which amplified the light fifty thousand times.

The result was a sharp, clear, red-tinted image when viewed through the binocular eyepiece. Mounted on the Commando, the cross-hair grid wasn't much use, because the Colt just wasn't that accurate over a long distance, although its killing range was nearly two hundred meters.

But it was a great weapon for close-quarters bush work, which was exactly why Hawker had selected it.

If he could see them through the scope, there was no doubt in his mind that he could get close enough to reach them with the Colt.

If Galway and Phelan came.

Hawker checked the safety on the Colt. He lifted the eyepiece of the night-vision scope to his cheek and scanned the tree-line along the wrought iron border that fenced Hayes's estate.

Finally, he spotted Megan. She sat high in a maple on her own deer stand.

A charge of warm emotion moved through him.

He wondered how she felt. Cold? And what was she thinking about? Him?

Night after night, it had been the same. Sitting alone in a tree. Able to see her but not able to go to her. Able to call to her but not touch her.

In a way, it was the perfect metaphor for their whole relationship.

But that would change, once her mission was over.

He hoped.

Hawker stiffened. A cone of white light fanned over the

horizon. A car was coming. He ducked back into the leaves and watched its approach through the Star-Tron. The scope turned the headlights to glowing rubies.

It was a police car. On patrol. It whooshed past doing a bored forty miles an hour.

Hawker smiled and wondered how many long, long nights he had spent doing just what the two cops in the car were doing. Talking. Shooting the bull. Listening to the static voice of the dispatcher on the radio.

Did he miss it?

Yeah. Maybe.

But the work he was doing now was a lot more important.

And that was consolation enough.

Hawker settled back against the trunk of the oak tree. The wind freshened. The moon glowed through the clatter of falling leaves. From off Lake Michigan came the pleasant hum of boat engines.

A cruiser out late. On a cold, September night. Hawker didn't envy them.

He checked his watch. It was 3:25 A.M.

The need for sleep moved through him like a fog. He reached for the Thermos of coffee and poured the plastic cup full. He had had the Thermos filled with *café con leche* at a Cuban restaurant.

The coffee was hot and strong and sweet.

Hawker lounged back, filled with his own thoughts. He finished the coffee and poured another half cup.

As he sipped the coffee, he reviewed the entire Bas Gan Sagart affair. It was like a cheap jigsaw puzzle. With pieces missing.

Hawker couldn't get the missing pieces out of his mind. They were like shards of glass in his brain.

They dug at him and nagged him. He was missing something, but what in the hell was it?

He felt the same way he did when he met some old friend unexpectedly and just couldn't remember the old friend's name. The name would bang around in the back of his brain, stoutly refusing to step forward.

Now some missing bit of data was refusing to step forward.

What was it?

Hawker puzzled over it, growing increasingly anxious. He cursed himself and cursed his memory.

And then it hit him. It came at him as if down a long, thin tunnel. It was something Boone Chezick had said: "If they live on land, we can track them. And if we can track them, we can find them."

And something Megan had said, too: "I covered almost every street in Chicago and still couldn't find their house."

If they live on land . . .

"The bastards came by boat!" he whispered to himself.

Quickly, Hawker checked his watch. It was 3:45 A.M.

How long had it been since he'd heard the humming sound of boat engines?

Twenty minutes? Twenty-five minutes?

Had it been long enough for them to send in a skiff?

Hawker swung down out of the tree and ran toward Megan's station. "Megan," he called to her in a hoarse whisper. "Stay here. I'm going up to the house."

"But why?" she called back sleepily. "What's wrong?"

"A boat. I heard a boat not far from here. I'm going to check—"

Hawker was interrupted by the sudden, heavy thud of gunfire. And then more gunfire.

Cursing himself, he ran through the darkness toward the mansion.

FIFTEEN

Hawker sprinted down the hill, legs pounding, arms driving, right fist holding the Colt Commando rifle like a lance.

He could see that more lights were on in the house now. What in the hell did that mean? Had Galway and Phelan made it inside?

If so, it could only mean one thing: Jacob Montgomery Hayes was dead. Or about to die.

And if he died, there was only one person to blame. Hawker. He couldn't have made it easier for those two psychopaths if he had tried. He had told Hayes to issue the challenge. He had told Hayes to keep the guard dogs locked up. And he had told Hayes to turn off all but a few lights so it would look as if everyone was asleep.

He had made bait of Hayes, and now the predators had struck while Hawker's brain slept.

If they live on land . . .

Why in the hell hadn't he thought of it before?

Hawker didn't stop sprinting when he reached the house.

Holding the Colt Commando on his hip, armed and ready, he circled the house at full speed.

And saw nothing.

Cautiously, he approached Hayes's study window. All the lights were on. He could see the high library shelves stacked with books and the red leather furniture and the glass cases filled with mounted insect and marine specimens.

He saw something else, too.

Far off in the corner, from behind Hayes's desk, protruded the shoes and lifeless legs of a dead man.

"*Shit!*" Hawker hissed.

He ran to the front of the house and tested the massive double doors. As they swung wide, he ducked through, the automatic rifle scanning the same line as his eyes.

From the hall outside Hayes's study, he heard the indistinct timbre of men's voices.

Quietly, he moved toward them. At the hall entrance, he hugged the wall, then jumped suddenly toward the voices.

"Freeze!" he yelled.

The hall light was on, too. Two men stood before him. At the first sound of his voice, their eyes grew wide with concern and they each swung their hand guns toward him.

Just as quickly, their faces relaxed.

"How nice of you to call," Hendricks, the butler, said in a deadpan dry voice.

Jacob Montgomery Hayes wasn't smiling. "We got one of them, Hawk. Hendricks planted a little room-to-room listening system, just in case they got past you. They got in through the coal bin and came up through the basement."

"A simple precaution," said Hendricks. "But effective. Unfortunately, two of the nasty buggers got away."

"*Two* got away?" said Hawker, surprised.

Through the front door, Megan Parnell came running. The grim look on her face changed immediately to a smile when she saw the three men standing in the hall.

"Ah, I'm so glad," she said in her soft Irish lilt. "You're not dead, are you?"

"A searing bit of insight, young lady," observed Hendricks. It was the first time Hawker had ever seen him smile.

She hesitated, then fell into Hawker's arms, hugging him warmly. "They got one of them, Megan. They said two got away. Come on, I want you to take a quick look at the body."

"And then what, James?"

"And then we go after the other two."

Hendricks and Hayes had shot the man as he came through the study door. Two clean shots: one in the face; another high and to the right of the breastbone.

There was no doubt he was dead.

A window at the far wall was shattered, and a line of splintered wood at eye level behind the desk told them that fire had been exchanged. But probably fearing an even worse trap, the other two had fled before their job was done.

"Is it Galway or Phelan?" Hawker demanded.

"Neither," she said. "I've never seen him before."

Through the broken window came the high buzz of a small outboard being started. Hayes gave Hawker a questioning look.

"They came in by boat," Hawker said. "A cruiser most of the

way, then probably paddled to shore in a skiff. We need a boat, Jacob. Give me anything that will float, and I'll go after them."

"*We'll* go after them," Megan insisted. She was no longer smiling.

"We keep a crash launch in the boat house," Hendricks sputtered. "The engine's in proper order, but it's on davits, and I hardly think—"

"Let's go!" Hawker called, already running. "And Jacob—if we're not back in an hour, get some help."

The "crash launch" was a thirteen-foot Boston Whaler with a forty-horsepower Johnson engine. It was a stubby projectile on davits beneath the roof of the boat house.

A steady northeast wind swept across Lake Michigan. It blew thigh-high breakers into the pilings, then sprayed them over the dock.

Hawker's pants became soaked while he wasted a long minute hunting for a hand crank to lower the boat into the water. Finally, he realized the davits worked off an electric motor. A moment later, he found the switch. The little boat settled itself on the black chop, lifting and rising like a duck.

"Wait until I get her started before you loosen the lines," Hawker yelled above the noise of the waves.

The Johnson fired to life, sputtered, then stalled. Forcing himself to remain calm, Hawker pumped the fuel-flow ball on the gas line. He pushed the starter key in to choke it, then tried again.

The engine roared and held.

"Jump in!"

Unclamping the bow cable, Megan stepped on as Hawker steered them out of the boat house. Lake Michigan was so rough that waves immediately broke over the bow. Hawker turned and pulled out the two scupper plugs so the boat could drain.

"Megan," he called, "you'd better sit back here with me. You'll get beaten to death up there. I've got to get her on plane, or we're going to swamp."

The woman moved nimbly over the center seat and edged in close to Hawker. She was trembling.

"Cold?" he asked.

"No," she said with a nervous laugh. "Scared."

Hawker put his arm around her and touched his lips to her smooth cheek. "No matter what happens," he said into her ear, "I want you to remember something. I love you, Megan."

Her eyes searched his in the darkness. "And I love you, James," she whispered. "Someday, you will know how much—I promise."

As he kissed her lips, she turned quickly away. "Not now," she said. "Later. Later, we'll talk."

"More than talk—and I'm going to hold you to it," said Hawker as he slid the Colt Commando into her arms. "Now, have a look through the night-vision scope. Scan the water. Slowly. What do you see?"

"The boat!" she exclaimed. "No, two boats! A wee tiny one, and a bigger one farther out."

"Which way?"

She began to wave her free hand, directing him. Hawker caught her arm. "The bow of the boat is at twelve o'clock," he said. "Just to port is eleven o'clock. Just to starboard is one o'clock. That's the way you're going to have to direct me."

"Halfway between twelve o'clock and one o'clock!"

"Twelve-thirty it is. Hold on!"

Hawker buried the throttle forward, and the Whaler dolphined out of the water, then settled on plane. Hawker quartered the waves as best he could, but every breaker still slammed against the hull with the impact of a sledgehammer.

"Let me know if we're gaining on them, Megan."

"I . . . I can't see anything! We're banging around too much—wait a minute! I just saw them. They're about halfway to the cruiser!"

"We've got to get there before they do. They can't hear us while their outboard is running, and they probably won't be able to see us—unless they have a scope like ours. If they do, we're sitting ducks."

The woman was still struggling to keep her eye pressed against the scope. "James, *we're going to catch them*. We're getting so close . . . should we be this close?"

Immediately, Hawker backed off on the throttle. He took the Colt Commando from her and looked through the Star-Tron.

He could see the cruiser, maybe half a mile away. It was a silhouette rolling on black water. Maybe forty feet long. A cabin that swept clear to the stern deck. A fly bridge atop the superstructure. It showed no lights.

It took him longer to find the skiff. He was shocked at how close they were. Another two or three minutes of running, and the Whaler would have run right over them.

The skiff was a tiny painter with a small sea gull-sized kicker.

Two hulking figures sat hunched in the boat. They were having a hell of a time fighting their way through the choppy water.

As close as they were, Hawker could just barely hear the droning bee-whine of the engine.

For that, he was glad.

The wind and waves were doing a good job of covering sound.

Quickly, Hawker calculated the best way to get the cruiser between them and the little painter.

He jammed the throttle forward, and the Whaler jumped onto plane, throwing a curtain of water over them.

Hawker ran for about five minutes, taking seas flush off the starboard beam, then cut suddenly northeast. The smacking of hull against waves rattled their teeth as he ran directly into the wind.

When he could see the cruiser directly off the Whaler's beam, he veered southeast toward the anchored yacht. It still showed no lights, but that didn't mean it was unattended. Fifty yards away, Hawker throttled the Whaler back as they idled toward the dark hulk before them.

"Keep your weapon ready," he ordered Megan as he brought the Whaler alongside. "At the first sign of any movement, don't hesitate. Open fire."

"With pleasure," she said in a tone Hawker had never heard from her before.

The seas rolled past the cruiser, doing their best to smash the two fiberglass hulls together. Alternately punching ahead and backing off on the throttle, Hawker finally put them close enough to tie the Whaler's bowline off on the cruiser's beam cleat.

He pulled himself up onto the deck of the boat. He motioned

for Megan to wait as he made a quick trip through the cabin, his automatic rifle ready.

When he was sure there was no one else aboard the boat, he helped the woman up and pulled her along into the control station of the deck salon. Hawker found the toggle switches that he hoped would give power to the deck lights.

"When they get here, don't open fire until I say," Hawker whispered. "I want a chance to talk to them, if I can."

"They didn't give my sister a chance, James!" she snapped nervously.

Hawker squeezed her arm tenderly. "Relax," he said. "It's almost over."

The high-pitched whine of the little outboard drew closer and closer. There was a dull thud as the painter smacked against the stern of the yacht. Hawker's hand grew tight on the Colt Commando as he heard the sound of men's voices.

Then they pulled themselves over the transom: two burly, hulking shapes arguing in thick Irish accents.

In one swift motion, Hawker flipped on the deck lights and charged them with the brutal-looking automatic poised at their heads.

"*Freeze!*" he yelled. "Don't move an inch, or you're dead!"

As the two men swung around in surprise, Hawker took one more confident step toward them, then stopped.

The shock moved through him like a cold, cold wind. It roared in his ears, and made him feel strangely dizzy.

The linebacker-sized man with the feral eyes and flaming red hair had to be Thomas Galway, the vicious leader of Bas Gan Sagart.

Hawker didn't have to speculate on the identity of the other man. Although his brain refused to believe it, there was no doubt who it was.

He looked wet and weary and vaguely embarrassed.

"Good evening, James," said Jimmy O'Neil. "Shall we drop our weapons, James?" He looked at Galway. "Yes, Thomas. I think he wants us to drop our weapons." His eyes returned to Hawker, and he smiled. "It's just what a good policeman would do, James."

SIXTEEN

"Jimmy," whispered Megan in disbelief. "But you . . . you were—"

"Dead?" he offered. "Not true, dear Megan. I'm sorry." His laugh was a mixture of sheepishness and disgust. "And I'm becoming increasingly sorry."

"But how?" Hawker demanded. "How in the hell did you get out of that fire? Someone damn well died that night, O'Neil—"

"It was the much-deserving Padraic Phelan," O'Neil said. "You see, my friend Galway here, Phelan, and a vanload of their goons came by the Ennisfree that night. I considered it quite fortunate that only I heard them come to the door. You and Megan were talking, you see." He looked at the brooding Galway, who stood drenched on the heaving deck. "Going to do a bit of fire-bombing, weren't you, Thomas?" O'Neil said.

"Shut up, Jimmy!" he barked. "Don't be saying another word to these two, damn it."

"But it's over, Thomas. Can't you see that?" He turned back to Hawker. "I went out into the street to meet them, James. That's why I hurried away so suddenly. Phelan was the supposed explosives 'expert' for the job that night, and he had built the bomb inside a briefcase. When I went outside to meet them, Phelan insisted he needed a drink. Against my direct orders, he made a quick trip into the bar for a bottle." O'Neil smiled. "Through more great good fortune, he carried the briefcase with him. I don't know what happened. None of us knew. Maybe he dropped the damn briefcase. In any case, Phelan was obviously not the explosives expert he pretended to be, because the bomb went off while he was inside. An accident, you see?

"I quickly saw that it was the perfect opportunity for me to go underground. A 'dead' Jimmy O'Neil could do a great deal more for the cause then a live, high-profile Jimmy O'Neil—in Chicago, anyway."

"You were working with Bas Gan Sagart all along!" Megan shouted.

"For the cause, dear Megan. Don't you understand?" O'Neil's fists clenched, and for a moment the old fire Hawker remembered so well returned to his eyes. "For once, I had the chance to make a lot of money for the cause. More money than we ever dreamed of—and damn it, I took that chance!"

"But they tried to kill you, too—that night at your house," Hawker insisted, still unwilling to believe that his close friend had involved himself with such scum.

O'Neil chuckled wearily. "Those were two of Thomas's goons, James. They followed you from Beckerman's place. My name was on that little note in case they got into trouble and needed a safe house. But the dumb bastards didn't know me from Adam. They were just two more of Thomas's trained killers." He gave Galway an evil, uneven grin. "Isn't that true, Thomas? Of course. You see, Megan, only my share of the money went to the IRA. But Thomas is a greedy little bastard—aren't you, Thomas?"

O'Neil looked at Hawker. "I've been a fool, James. A fool right along. And I'm glad you've caught us. I deserve whatever sentence the courts choose to give me—and they will, because I'm going to tell them everything." He winked playfully at Thomas Galway, who was scowling. "Be quite a story, won't it, Thomas, lad? I'll get a long stay in the pen, but you"—O'Neil laughed—"but you'll get the bloody chair!"

"Will I?" Galway yelled with a maniacal gleam in his eye. He touched his back pocket, and the stocky, snub-barreled revolver appeared in his hand so quickly, Hawker didn't have time to move. Galway backhanded O'Neil with the butt of the weapon, then Hawker saw the barrel spout fire.

In the same instant, there was a jarring impact against his right arm. The slug knocked Hawker to the ground and sent his Colt Commando spinning. Through the first wave of pain and shock, Hawker watched Megan launch herself at Galway like a tigress. She landed on his right shoulder, clawing at his face and neck. Her fingers found his left eye.

He gave a tortured scream as she dug his eye away from his face. O'Neil got shakily to his feet and drew back his fist as if to hit Galway.

But the revolver exploded again, and O'Neil tumbled backward, his head spouting blood.

Hawker rolled toward his automatic weapon. He grasped it in his left hand and whirled just in time to see Galway dig the revolver into Megan's chest and fire. She screamed once and collapsed onto the deck.

"You bastard!" Hawker heard some distant voice yell, a voice that was his own. He fought his way to his feet and brought the Commando to bear on Galway's throat.

Just before Hawker fired, there was a microsecond of great clarity, as if in slow motion. And in that second, it seemed he could see it all, as if from above—the four of them on the heaving cruiser as Lake Michigan swept past, black and cold. Jimmy O'Neil, his best friend who had forfeited that which he held most sacred for the beloved cause—his honor. Megan Parnell, the passionate celibate of haunting beauty, who never lost her curious air of nobility. Even now. As she lay dying.

And Thomas Galway. In that microsecond before Hawker fired, it seemed he could see Galway most clearly of all. The long, matted red hair. The vicious look of the hunted animal on his face. The furrows of blood Megan's nails had plowed through his cheek, and the dangling eyeball she had dug from its socket.

As Galway brought the revolver up to shoot him a second time, Hawker's left fist squeezed the trigger of the Colt Commando.

Galway jolted backward, his body jerking in spasms as the heavy-caliber slugs poured through it.

Still holding the trigger down, Hawker walked toward Galway. The hatred was like a madness in him now. Galway's body was like a receptacle through which to pour his anger.

When the Colt's twenty-round clip was empty, Hawker smashed the weapon down onto the bloodied corpse, then knelt quickly beside Megan Parnell.

He felt her dark sweater soaked with blood as he cradled her in his arms.

"Megan," Hawker whispered, his voice a weak sob in the whistle of wind. *Megan . . .*

Her eyes fluttered open and focused slowly on him. Her mouth formed a weak smile. "James? Oh, thank God you're not hurt. I thought he killed you."

"He's dead, Megan. Galway and—and Jimmy, too. It's just us now, Megan. You've completed your mission."

Her muscles contracted with a spasm of pain as she reached up and traced the outline of his lips with her index finger. "Am I dying, James?"

"No," he lied, his voice choking.

Her smile broadened. "It's such a bad liar, you are. But it doesn't matter, for I'm dying with the first peace I've known in a very long time. I'm only sorry to be leaving you."

Hawker hugged her close. "Don't talk," he whispered. "The boat has to have a VHF radio. I'm going to call for a Coast Guard helicopter—"

"Don't," she whispered. "Please don't leave me." Her breathing was heavier now, and Hawker could see that she had to struggle to keep her eyes open. "I want to spend these last moments with you, for I've loved you for so very long, though you didn't even know it—"

"I knew, Megan. I knew."

"But you couldn't have known, James. For I've loved you since I heard the stories about your family on me own mother's knee. Direct descendants of Cuchulain, the great warrior legend of Ulster, they said you were." Her sweet laughter became a choking cough.

"For God's sake, don't talk, Megan," he pleaded.

"But I must, James," she whispered. "I must tell you why I feel the way I do. The stories were so lovely to hear, you see. The stories about your handsome, dashing father who broke a hundred hearts, and then took revenge on the Orangemen who murdered his entire family but one. You, James. Don't you see? Don't you understand why my love for you—"

Hawker kissed her lips tenderly, trying to force her to stop talking, to stop wasting precious time—and her own fading energy.

Even so, she continued. "... why my love for you could not be the way you wanted it to be—yes, and the way I wanted it to be?"

Her blue eyes grew alive and warm as she pulled his head toward hers for a final, dry kiss. And the next words she spoke were to echo in Hawker's head for the endless trip back to shore, and the endless years to come.

"James, how can you be so bright and so slow at the same time?" The smile she was to die with returned to her lips as her small hand closed tightly over Hawker's. "Can't you understand, my darling, that my mother was one of the many whose hearts were broken by your father, though he never knew it. James . . . dear, dear James . . . I'm your sister. . . ."

ABOUT THE AUTHOR

Randy Wayne White was born in Ashland, Ohio, in 1950. Best known for his series featuring retired NSA agent Doc Ford, he has published over twenty crime fiction and nonfiction adventure books. White began writing while working as a fishing guide in Florida, where most of his books are set. His earlier writings include the Hawker series, which he published under the pen name Carl Ramm. White has received several awards for his fiction, and his novels have been featured on the *New York Times* bestseller list. He was a monthly columnist for *Outside* magazine and has contributed to several other publications, as well as lectured throughout the United States and travelled extensively. White currently lives on Pine Island in South Florida, and remains an active member of the community through his involvement with local civic affairs as well as the restaurant Doc Ford's Sanibel Rum Bar and Grill.

HAWKER EBOOKS

FROM OPEN ROAD MEDIA

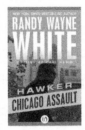

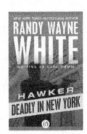

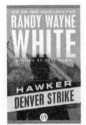

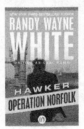

Available wherever ebooks are sold

OPEN ROAD
INTEGRATED MEDIA

Open Road Integrated Media is a digital publisher and multimedia content company. Open Road creates connections between authors and their audiences by marketing its ebooks through a new proprietary online platform, which uses premium video content and social media.

CPSIA information can be obtained at www.ICGtesting.com
Printed in the USA
BVOW08s0612100516

447483BV00001B/4/P